a red tale

nicola mar

Copyright © 2014 by Nicola Mar

ISBN: 978-0-991-51899-9 (paperback)
ISBN: 978-0-991-51891-3 (ebook)

Marworks Publishing
Printed in the United States of America

First Edition

For my mother Cathy,
who is with me always.

"To improve is to change; to be perfect is to change often."

Winston Churchill

PROLOGUE

THE AFTERNOON sunlight beamed through the windows in the museum. Particles of the dry earth and salty sea lingered in the air, floating as if held by no gravity. The room smelled of rust and mildew, but I barely noticed as I looked up in amazement at the bones that towered over me. Their sharp, jagged edges stood still in the air as if they were petrified in motion. I could almost sense the creature's age from its remains.

The museum curator walked over and shook hands with my mother and father as if he thought they had killed the beast. He ran his fingers over the dusty plaque next to the animal before he cleared his throat and proceeded to read the inscription out loud. "A newly discovered aquatic species, water dragons—also known as Wayters—are believed to have formed from their ancient ancestors, the Plesiosaurs. Their fan-shaped tails make them capable of swimming at more than 75mph." Then he nodded as if he already knew Pa's question. "Caught right here by Parrot Pond beach in St. Michael. Golly, this little Caribbean island has gotten a lot of tourism because of it."

I sat on Pa's back; my small feet dangled over his shoulders as I watched Mama lean her head back and laugh nervously.

"You think it's real?" she asked Pa quietly, glancing up at me to see if I was listening.

I saw some sort of curiosity in her face but not enough for her to ever consider that dragons could be living on the Earth's surface—in the past, present, or future.

"Of course it's real," the assertive caretaker said loudly. "It's only a matter of time before they're eating up all of us humans. They ain't got nothing left in the ocean." He paraded back to his post by the blue whale, an animal much bigger than the dragon, although not nearly as fascinating.

"It was caught only three years ago. Presumably the Wayters are coming ashore," said Pa, opening his eyes to match his wide grin.

As I looked at the old bones, I pictured myself on top of the skeleton, riding it like a horse. I pretended that the dragon came alive with scales on its rough skin and with eyes the color of burning coal. In my mind, its tail spun around, releasing red colors that made a rainbow-like effect in the air.

I quickly pushed my head over Pa's so that I was in his view, before declaring, "They're coming. It's too cold in the water now. They can't survive." The words came rushing out of my mouth from somewhere I didn't recognize. The unsolicited knowledge flew through me like I was just a vehicle to its freedom.

"Gotta keep our eyes out for the water dragons," Pa said to me in a singsong voice, as if I had no idea what I was saying.

CHAPTER 1

THE SUN shone through the tiny airplane window, blinding me. Far below, the snow-covered islands of the West Indies were like stars on the American flag—white, irregular shapes littered on an unmoving, blue canvas. The thin, stringy clouds mixed with pink colors that shot across the sky. They whisked by very quickly as heavy winds shook the plane. The little boy behind me had his face glued to the circular window, kicking my seat and screaming each time he could see the island. Every time I felt his foot hit my back, I jumped as last night's nightmares about water dragons tumbled around in my mind.

The plane bumped over the thick air and little by little I could make out the familiar surroundings of my home. The rolling hills came into view, followed by the bright colored houses. I recognized the tiny airport with its worn out landing strip just above the light blue ocean. Usually I'd see people watching the planes and the sandy beaches full of colorful towels, but today, all I saw was white snow. There was not a soul in sight. The small Rasta colored beach bar that was usually booming with activity was boarded up and desolate.

My hands gripped tightly around my seat cushion as people gasped with anxiety as the plane descended. The wings went up, the wheels came down, and the captain prepared us for a fast landing. "It was a pleasure having you on board, folks. Welcome to St. Michael. We know you have a choice in air travel and we appreciate you choosing to fly with Caribbean Airways. Enjoy your stay."

Home, sweet home! I thought as people looked on in fright.

As soon as I cleared customs, I squeezed through the crowd of awaiting passengers, until finally, I spotted Mama. Her brown hair was parted to the right side, as usual. She was wearing one of her ankle length dresses, but a big, brown jacket covered most of it. Seeing her caused a sigh of relief, and I suddenly felt relaxed. The nightmares dissipated from my mind. Classes were over. I was home. The three long years of learning about water dragons had been exhausting.

"Anastasia," my mother called, waving her arms in the air. I cringed at the sound of my full name. No one, not even my father, had called me anything but Stasia since I was born. "I missed you!" Mama threw her long, pale arms around me and hugged me harder than anyone had in a long time. My mother, whose skin was always sun-kissed, had lost her beautiful tan. "So? How was the big city of Puncchit?" she asked, as if I'd only been there for a one-week vacation. "Well, you're not going to like this weather. They are predicting even more snow tonight!" she said quickly, changing the subject before I could answer.

"More snow predicted in Puncchit too. Good thing Pa stocked up on food and water," I assured her. Puncchit News had done another special on global cooling a couple nights ago. Despite the definite theories of global warming years ago, scientists were now scrambling to come up with an excuse for their blatant miscalculations. The interview showed a scientist who had, about three years ago, claimed to have been studying global warming for decades and who'd insisted that the period of colder winter weather was just a fluke. The whole interview was mocked as we now knew the winter was lasting longer than just one season, and tropical climates were experiencing freezing weather. It'd been three years since snow started falling in the winter in St. Michael, an island that had always been warm year-round.

"How's he holding up without BreadBar?" Mama asked rhetorically, clearly aware that Pa always went crazy when his food truck was shut down on snowy days.

"You know he misses you," I said, relieving her worry. Her expression lightened.

"He didn't tell me when he'd be back. Shouldn't take too long to wrap up everything in the apartment," Mama said, meeting my eyes directly as if it were a question.

I shrugged, and then nodded confidently.

Mama hugged me one more time before wrapping her hand around my bag. "Welcome to paradise. Remember, you always wanted a white Christmas on St. Michael. Looks like you're going to have one!"

Small groups rushed from inside the airport to their cars. Hooded jackets covered their faces and greetings were quick. It wasn't how I remembered the laid-back feeling of the Caribbean, where everyone was drinking beer, smiling, dancing, and being carefree. Instead, people maneuvered around the heaps of brown, slushy snow that was raked to the corners of the parking lot where only two taxis were parked. Our truck was one of the only other vehicles in the parking lot. When Mama hit the unlock button, I rushed to it and swung my suitcase in the back seat.

On the way home, the truck bounced in and out of potholes. Once we got out of the airport, there were no more big hotels or tall buildings. We ventured into the "unknown" as the tourists called it. We passed little shacks made from scraps of aluminum sheets, wood, branches of palm trees and other unwanted materials. On the brink of collapse, one hurricane would take their existence off the map.

But even people in proper homes struggled. Few had heat on the island. I saw people burning large fires in metal barrels. Candles lined their windows. Goats and cows were still tied up to trees, freezing. Starving.

It would have looked like séances to a visitor.

Then we passed the sugar cane fields. Plantation workers were completely put out of business by global cooling. The only things said to remain in these fields were the ghosts of the owners who starved to death when the most important crop in St. Michael was demolished.

And finally, after miles and miles of barren fields covered in snow, we reached Parrot Pond, the small neighborhood of houses that surrounded a secluded inlet from the ocean. It was named not after the bird, but after the small parrotfish that were frequently seen swimming in the channel. I stared through the frosty windshield at the icy pond and the snowy hill in front of us. It looked too dangerous to travel on. Mama put the old truck into 4-wheel drive and the tires immediately spun as she floored the gas petal.

"I just hate driving this old thing. Your father insisted on getting this big truck." She struggled with the clutch, jerking her body from side to side. Driving never was her strong suit. The beat up truck started to move and we slowly drove up the steep slope. The house came into view. The tarnished black cast iron gate that opened into the yard had icicles dangling between the spaces.

"Home, sweet home!" Mama said as we both alighted from the truck. I struggled to carry my suitcase over the wet ground. The beautiful stone courtyard my parents were so proud of was completely covered in snow. It could have been a slab of concrete.

When the weather changed for the season, it changed quickly. Mama said that St. Michael had gotten its first snow in December of the year I had left for Puncchit. Now, three years later, it had already begun snowing in September.

Everything looked different in the yard and it was throwing me off. The outdoor barbeque grill was missing, probably brought inside. The umbrella on the table was not open. There was no fruit, leaves, or flowers on the trees. There were far *less* trees. The pots were empty. The "Welcome to the Forrester's" sign was partially covered in snow. We were now the Ester family and you were not welcomed but "omed". The winter weather looked far less beautiful here but maybe that was just my resentment talking; snow did not belong in the Caribbean.

Near the front door, something else caught my detective eye—fresh animal tracks neatly pressed into the snow.

"Who do you think these are from, Mama?" I asked, hunching over to take a closer look.

"I really haven't come across an animal in our yard in weeks. I figured they'd all died, or were hibernating. Maybe feral cats?" She looked up and cocked her head to the side before she continued walking. "I wonder what they are eating these days," she mumbled to herself.

I followed the footprints closely. They were gently pressed one in front of the other in an almost straight line. I could see the pattern of bones. They were a lot bigger than a cat's paw; I just knew I had seen them somewhere before. The long, narrow toes. The uneven skin pattern. The diamond shaped pads. Dragons!

"Dragons, Mama!"

She didn't bother turning around. "You're brainwashed now." She dug her feet in the snow, messing up the footprints completely. "You know, those iguanas have become quite resilient. Yes, that's who they are probably from," she said, convincing herself.

I unzipped my carry-on bag and pulled out the "dragon gloves" Pa had given me before classes started in Puncchit. They were red and looked exactly like mittens, but Pa said they could ward off evil and make every water dragon become friendly. I followed the remaining tracks closely, hovering the dragon gloves above them. They went all the way up to the front door where they disappeared.

That's strange, I thought. *I wonder where it went...*

The familiar scent of 'home' distracted me as Mama opened the wooden door that led into the bright kitchen. Sunlight washed the countertops with a white glow.

"It's good to be back. No matter what the temperature is!" I said, giving Mama a large, one-sided smile. There were even freshly made brownies on a plate and a glass of iced milk.

"Your favorite," Mama said. "Bring one to the dragon when you find it, okay?" She went straight to the coffee maker to brew herself a cappuccino while I looked out the window contemplating how global cooling had come so quickly. It was only a few years ago that St. Michael was warm in the winter months. Now it looked like Puncchit outside. But there was one difference. It was quiet. We didn't have neighbors around. We didn't have fire truck sirens wailing, cabs honking, and cars speeding. There were no kids screaming in the apartment below, or people enjoying the rooftop lounge above. I could sense my body starting to relax and my thoughts became clearer and clearer. It was almost like I could hear my mind talking. It told me to go to my room, so I grabbed a brownie and proceeded to the old attic—my bedroom.

The wooden stairs creaked and bent as I slowly made my way up, stopping to admire all the paintings on the wall and reminiscing about the good memories attached to them. Mama had painted all of them. Some were bright and colorful; others were gray and somber—a smorgasbord of different feelings and emotions. Some were still stacked in corners, never hung. When I opened my bedroom door, I could see that the bed was neatly made. Mama's old photographs that I'd collected hung on the walls. Black and white photos of strangers were interesting to me. Their dark eyes peered out from the paper as if they were trying to tell me something. Together the people all stood, expressionless, but I could tell that there was love there because they all held hands. Draped on the windows to block out the sunlight were red and purple curtains I'd bought in a thrift shop. The light shone through, but only slightly, giving the room a deep reddish color. Never mind how they smelled.

I cracked open the louvered window and breathed in deeply. No matter what the temperature was, the ocean breeze still filled the air. I loved the smell of sea air. It reminded me of being a child on the beach with wet hair and sandy feet, and the warm ocean I used to spend hours, days and months playing in. My parents claimed that I'd always known how to swim. They can't remember how or when I learned; maybe it was instinctual, engrained in my genes.

Out the window, different colors formed in the sky as the sun went down. Reds, oranges, and pinks shot across the horizon dipping into the blue sea like one of Mama's paintings. There was really no other sight like the sun setting over the ocean. I took a moment to enjoy it before I lit three candles and sat on my old bed. It squeaked and rattled. I threw my socks in the corner. My sweater went next. I was suddenly so tired from all the traveling, the classes, the reading, and the homework. The candlelight flickered red images of dancing dragons in front of my closed eyelids, and I began to relax by counting backwards...

Ninety-nine...

Ninety-eight...

Ninety-seven...

Unwind. I kept repeating the word in my mind.

Ninety-six...

Ninety-five...

Ninety...four...

I could feel my body numbing.

CHAPTER 2

ANOTHER WORLD came alive as my eyes closed and my brain ventured into dreamland. My mind took me through the formation in a matter of seconds as information was given to me at lightning speed.

Four thousand five hundred years ago, a place was formed under the ocean called Surritz; it was the result of many years of air being trapped below the ocean surface. For some reason, certain particles of the air had been resistant to the usual laws of science; instead of rising to the surface of the water, they had stayed beneath it. They'd wandered along under the ocean until they found each other and joined to create an air bubble. As the air bubble grew, sucking in more and more oxygen, it started to sink miles downward until it hit the ocean's floor. Slowly, from that point forward, particles of life were drawn in from the water until they began to grow. Life started to materialize. The conditions were so perfect that plants developed into animals, and animals into human beings.

The people of Surritz were self-sufficient beings who used the vast energy of the sea to foresee the future and re-create the past. Animals and people co-existed peacefully in this place as one had developed from the other. There were rolling green hills in all directions and the most colorful wild flowers anyone could think of. Freshwater, distilled from the ocean, ran through the land in streams, supplying the people with all the drinking water they needed. There was one tall waterfall and the faint sound of falling water could always be heard throughout the land.

It was nothing like the Earth I knew. Water dragons were the most abundant species on the island. They helped the people with their daily activities–getting their food, making decisions, building things, and even developing their emotions. Some had the ability to heal people, some to help people, and others to provide knowledge. But, Surritz did not remain this way. Something happened that changed its destiny.

My water-powered alarm clock jolted me awake. *What happened to Surritz?* I slammed the button on the clock, spilling water on my hand. Shutting my eyes quickly, I hoped to continue the dream. But the clock kept gurgling, fighting to wake me up. It slowly suctioned water up its tubes to the top of the waterfall before letting the liquid explode down the rocks to hit the pond below. As usual, it halted for a few seconds repeating the same sound as if it were choking. But faithfully every time, it coughed up what was trapping the stream and the flow continued.

I slowly became aware of my body again. The dream lingered in my mind as I pulled back the dark drapes and glanced out the window, hoping I'd been transplanted to Surritz like Dorothy to Oz. But I hadn't. As I slowly moved my limbs, I saw the colors in the ocean as the sun rose.

In my suitcase I found the dragon gloves again, along

with the three snowsuits I'd packed. I hung them up in the closet along with my boots, hats, and everything else for winter. On the shelf were books Mama always tried to get me to read, but they were still sealed in plastic, unopened. *Tales of St. Michael* was on the top. Pa had bought it for me so I could learn a little bit more about the local island culture. I thought about reading it today, but since the warm weather picture on the front cover didn't apply to right now, I figured the stories were useless. I piled on the winter clothing before heading outside.

As I walked out the front door reminiscing about warmer times, something caught my eye. I ignored the iridescent clouds of breath that leaked through my lips because I spied something more interesting: the same animal tracks I saw yesterday. The animal must have just come by! The wooden wind chime in the garden sang to me as I followed the tracks from the front door towards the driveway. Snow collapsed under my boots making it hard to walk. I zipped my coat higher until it pinched my neck and I began breathing heavily as I drudged through the snow past the car, balancing on parts of the ground that were rock hard. The streets were not plowed and I couldn't tell where the driveway ended and the road began.

The paw prints were big and fork-like, taking a straight line down the road. Maybe it *was* an iguana that had been coming to the house to find food. I wondered if it was trying to get inside, for the tracks only led to and from the front door. Gusts of wind blew the fresh snow off the top of the ground. I could hear it travel and disperse a few feet away only to be interrupted by my huffing and puffing. I pulled my scarf tighter around my mouth as I walked down the hill trying not to topple over. Just as I stopped to take a break, I heard animal squeals in the distance but I could not make out what animal it was. For a second, the squeals almost sounded like words.

Down the hill I ran until I was falling over in the snow. *Where was it coming from?* My boots sank deeper and deeper into the slush. I breathed heavily, panting.

As I neared the bottom of the hill, I looked out at the ocean. It moved slightly with the current, slowly rolling waves ashore, until they got larger and larger, taller and taller. Suddenly, dozens of clear scales were spit out of the ocean and blown around in the air as if they were combining to form life. Scream like noises whistled in the distance. I stopped twenty feet short of the ocean, astonished that the animal tracks were leading right into the water.

It all made sense. A Wayter that could endure the ocean temperature but came ashore just long enough to eat and then go back. But what was it looking for? My instincts did not say a human meal. My gut persuaded me to walk closer to the ocean, just to see what was going on, but my mind told me to run the other way.

Giving in to my mind's better judgment, I turned and quickly started back up the hill, my heart racing as if someone were chasing me. Thump, thump, it pounded quickly in my chest, fueled by the adrenaline that raced through my system. *I just need to get back. I need to get out of this cold.*

The wind picked up and pushed against me, prohibiting me from going back home. A hailstorm of cold, chafing air engulfed my whole body as I fell backwards. I got on my hands and knees and crawled like a child as snow blew against my chest and froze my arms. Extending my neck higher to avoid getting any more snow in my face, I fixated my eyes on the old truck in our driveway. It was only twenty feet away, but it seemed like miles as I crawled through a mini snowstorm.

"One step at a time. Just keep going," I mumbled. The ocean rumbled behind me and the wind howled in front of me. I was inching forward slowly but my body almost gave out as the cold air rushed into my lungs.

I didn't look back until I finally reached the car. When I did, the ocean was as calm and as still as a pond. It was quiet again. No snow moved because there was no wind. Even my tracks were barely visible anymore. I brushed the scales off my clothes and they fell quickly to the ground before the snow magically absorbed them.

Panicking and covered in wet slush, I ran inside, but Mama was too busy taking a pie from the oven to notice.

"Pumpkin pie?" she said, mimicking a southern accent.

"Maybe later. I'm going upstairs to change my clothes." My voice shook. I was not hungry at all, but my mouth still filled with saliva from the sweet scent of the freshly baked pie. The automatic reaction somehow brought me back into the present moment and I calmed down, knowing my mother was right there ready to feed me.

"Oh, Stasia, I wanted to show you," she said, pointing out the window. "You see it?"

"No, see what?" I said, confused, wondering if she had seen the ocean waves swell as if we were in the middle of a tropical storm.

"The green thing, in the tree. It's an iguana! I told you those creatures are tough as nails. They adapt, you know?" She was pleased with her find. She turned around, humming as she slowly cut through the warm pie, releasing more of the sweet pumpkin scented steam that danced freely under my nostrils.

CHAPTER 3

AN HOUR later, I was lying on my bed, in clean dry clothes, staring at the wood slaves that dotted the walls, still like cracks.

"Stasia, sweet pea, we are going to be late," Mama called up the stairs.

Mama was never, ever late.

"I'm coming." I got up and tousled my dirty blond hair, deciding whether I should get dressed up or go casual.

"It's only lunch, Stasia, at their house," Mama said as she saw me in my sundress. "Aren't you going to be cold?"

This was the first time I was seeing our family friend, Dr. Rose, in what felt like decades. His daughter was a good friend, but I had lost touch with her even before I moved to Puncchit. Amelie Rose, I thought to myself, wishing I had a prettier name. Stasia Forrester just didn't sound as poetic.

Amelie and her father had stayed on St. Michael when Pa and I moved to Puncchit, and Mama had met up with them occasionally over the years. According to Mama, Amelie hardly ever got out of the house, which bothered Dr. Rose. He didn't exactly know how to handle Amelie since her mother, his wife, had died five years ago.

"What if Amelie has changed? Just because we were friends when I was nine, doesn't mean we will still get along now. Six years is a long time. People change," I said to Mama, running down the stairs, which were so squeaky they spoke their own language.

But that wasn't my real concern. My true anxiety was because I was shy. I hadn't seen Amelie in years, but inside I was sure she was still the same friend I had in grade school.

"Don't worry so much. Grab your coat." She gestured to the table where I had thrown my mittens and scarf. They lay on the floor, but my jacket was neatly tucked around the back of a chair.

The ride to the Rose's took less than five minutes. The same half paved road took us to the top of the hill where their house towered over the ocean. It was a little smaller than ours, but the view made up for it. We parked the truck just behind Dr. Rose's gray Chevy. I recognized the car because it was the same one he'd had for the last ten years, only now, rust had eaten the sides and the paint was chipped at the corners.

Dr. Rose walked out the front door in a green parka, blue jeans, and black snow boots.

"Mayleen!" he cried, hugging Mama. She gave him two small kisses, one on each cheek.

"And who's this?" He winked at me, held up his hand for a high five, and gave me a tight hug. "Stasia Forrester. My, have you grown up!"

I smiled back awkwardly.

"Come in, come in. Let's get out of the cold."

He had re-furnished the entire house. Beautiful old wicker furniture and antique sea wood greeted us in the living room. The floors were a darker reddish mahogany color. He even had a fireplace now.

"Stasia, of course you remember Amelie," Dr. Rose motioned to his daughter who was walking out of the bedroom. I turned around to see a beautiful dark haired girl with giant blue eyes. *Did she have those blue eyes before? Guess I never noticed.*

"Getting older every time you see her, right Mayleen?" Dr. Rose joked to Mama.

Amelie greeted me with a perfect smile and a beautiful set of manicured red nails.

"Hi, Amelie. It's been a long time," I said, reluctant to hug her.

The last time I had seen Amelie she had short hair and braces. She used to be a little bubbly and unusually loud.

She lunged at me like a bear, wrapping her arms around my neck. "Hey Stasia! Been a long, long time."

"Lunch is almost ready. I made my family's secret pasta bolognese! Why don't you all have a seat and catch up," Dr. Rose pointed to the fancy table. I wondered if it was like our formal dining room table that no one ever used unless we had company.

"I'll help you in the kitchen, Henry," Mama replied, sounding cheerful.

"Thanks, Mayleen," Dr. Rose's voice trailed off into the other room.

Amelie and I sat down across from each other. She was about 5'6" with a very petite frame. I also remembered her as being a little chubby. She had grown out of that.

"How have you been Stasia? How's Puncchit? You gonna teach me what I need to know about the water dragons? Since I didn't attend classes and all." She dug her white teeth into a buttered roll. I couldn't help but notice how beautifully her teeth contrasted with her dark skin. She was much lighter than her father, but much darker than her mother was. A beautiful mix. "So what's up with all the hoopla? My father never told me why people were being forced to attend classes in Puncchit."

I looked around first to see if Mama was listening. I didn't want to ruin the good mood she was in. "You know the statue in town? The one of the prophet Baldamere?"

"Yeah. HE WHO HATH EARS TO HEAR, LET HIM HEAR," she sung in a deep voice, referencing the biblical inscription that was carved next to the monument.

"He predicted that water dragons would morph into air-breathing, land-walking creatures sometime in the 21st century."

Amelie laughed loudly and faked a scared expression.

"When the first water dragon skeleton was seen in a museum in St. Michael twelve years ago, government officials started to praise Baldamere and his statue was erected in the center of town. At that point, all teenagers who were living on Caribbean islands were forced to attend "dragon education classes" in their mother countries for three years. We go to Puncchit since it oversees the ruling of St. Michael. Kids there are taking the class just to learn about a new species, but for us it's about knowledge that can potentially protect us if we see them."

"I can't wait for the day they come ashore. Finally something interesting will happen on this boring island," Amelie said.

"Mama thinks it's madness. She doesn't believe in psychics. She gets mad every time my father talks about the dragons." I frowned.

"I'd actually love to go. Can't believe my father didn't send me."

"The law has been in place, but barely enforced until recently. Residents refused to travel when no one has actually seen a live Wayter. Mama says the classes are just a way to extort money."

"So what was it like? What did they have you do?"

"They had a 3D image of the skeleton that was here in the museum. We had to memorize almost every bone in its body! Just in case, I dunno, maybe it's not friendly. Maybe they eat humans, who knows," I said.

Amelie kept eating. "I can handle a Wayter. I've been doing some martial arts. Did I ever tell you about the time I was chased by a mongoose?"

"No," I said. "But mongooses don't attack humans. And aren't they relatively small?"

"That's not the point. Point is, I wasn't scared. They're slinking and slippery looking."

"They have fur," I added slowly.

"Slippery as in tube-like. You still are so literal, Stasia."

"Ok," I said dropping the subject. "What else is new on the island?" But I was still trying to picture a mongoose as a slippery, scary animal.

"Dad's practice is dying down since lots of people have moved off the island. You know I've been home schooled for the last few years, right?"

I didn't know. It wasn't something I ever thought was an option. But I was instantly jealous. "Why? I mean, don't you want to be around your friends?"

"Ugh. You know, not so much. Plus the government doesn't plow the streets in the winter, and we just can't get anywhere," she replied, still chewing.

Her personality was alive. There was nothing in her tone to suggest that she had ever been self-conscious in her life.

"What about food?" I asked, "I mean, what do you guys eat?"

I sounded like the kids in Puncchit who ignorantly asked about St. Michael like it was a different planet. I'd always lie and say we lived in trees, like monkeys, unaware of what or when our next meal would be.

The sad thing was that they believed me.

"We stock up on food every summer. The whole basement is filled with Spam!" She laughed, widening her eyes.

Spam. The word alone brought chills to my body. We all became quite accustomed to eating the canned meat for two months after a category five hurricane devastated the island six years ago. Hurricane Lee. It had been the twelfth storm of the season and it had hit us straight on.

"Well, we should hang out again," I said, remembering the time that it was warm enough for hurricanes to form.

"Yes, I would love to. I mean, you're only five minutes away and I can walk to your house." Her loud laugh filled the room.

Dr. Rose entered, holding a big dish of pasta. I guess they had some frozen pasta in the basement too!

"Bon appétit!" Mama declared. We all dug in like we hadn't had a home cooked meal in months.

"Mmmm, so good, Henry. Thank you," Mama said, glaring at me for a comment.

"Thanks Dr. Rose. It's delicious," I quickly added.

I couldn't help but think that if my father was dark like Dr. Rose, I'd be exotic and beautiful like Amelie. She was teased in school because of it but she had been so confident she never cared. Now I envied her for both her looks *and* her spirit.

"So how was dragon school Stasia? You make lots of new friends in Puncchit?" Dr. Rose asked, raising his wine glass to his pursed lips.

When I thought about it, all I seemed to remember was the young bullies teasing me about an ugly birthmark on my neck, calling me a giraffe because of my height, and calling me an animal because of my bushy, curly hair. Not that they were anything special themselves, but they traveled in packs and seemed to convince people they were worthy of being liked. If only I had Amelie's confidence, maybe I could have stayed off their radar.

I thought about Maisy Longwood, the only girl who had actually taken an interest in where I was from. She'd even expressed interest in coming to St. Michael. And Flynn Echoes, the cute boy who had actually spoken to me. I missed seeing him.

Deflecting the subject, I replied politely to Dr. Rose saying that I'd love to be schooled with Amelie, hoping to plant the homeschooling idea in Mama's head. The thought of never being around my peers again made me ecstatic.

"How's your dad? He still running BreadBar?" Red sauce stained his lips.

"Puncchities sure love their pastries," I replied semi-sarcastically.

"That's great. Anytime he wants to send down some Brooderkaas we'll be here!" He laughed. "Melted cheese and butter on bread…YUM. I do wish we could speak more on the phone. I miss that guy. You know, Amelie could use some time out of the house. Why don't you girls hang out? Even though it's cold, you could still take a walk down to the beach. I'm sure you miss the ocean, Stasia."

Dr. Rose said this with so much hope; it was like I could read the words on his face—he was terrified of raising a teenager all by himself. He had gotten more gray hair and had put on some weight since I had last seen him. His eyes had even lost some of their life. I could only imagine what he'd gone through since his wife died.

"Sure, yeah. I'd love to," I nodded to Amelie. "Come back to the house with us today."

"You'll teach me your dragon slaying moves?" she asked.

"Yeah, you won't learn them from a mongoose."

* * *

THE DEN was by far the nicest room in our house. It was six steps lower than the rest of the house. Because of the tall ceilings, books were lined on shelves almost to the top. More were stacked on the two coffee tables and even on the side chair across the room. A war was beginning to break out between the throw pillows and the books. In some places, books were balanced on the pillows, and in others the pillows triumphed on top of the books. Mama made one specific rule for the room—no noise. The rule was set in place after one occasion when I had asked if we could put a TV in the corner. Mama had been so insulted I felt like she may have disowned me.

"Guess it will snow hard again," I said to Amelie as I rested my feet on three stacked pillows. "I'm okay with being lazy. I'm still full from your dad's pasta."

She agreed.

"So, are you really being home schooled? How does that work? Does your father actually make you do anything?" I asked, trying not to sound too envious, although I was, extremely.

Amelie ran her hands through her shiny, straight hair, reluctant to reveal what was behind her slight smile. She looked up the stairs before replying and I instantly got the "uh-oh" feeling. *What was she up to?*

"Well, don't say anything, but I'm not really doing schoolwork." She coyly looked at me and I now realized that the old Amelie hadn't changed. She was always the one trying to do something she wasn't supposed to be doing. Even when we were seven years old, she had refused to let her mom comb her hair in the morning or pick out her clothes.

"So, you're not doing homework?" I was confused and even more jealous at the same time.

"I've been reading my Dad's psychology books instead. I'm going to be a doctor, too, so I might as well speed up the process right? I know more about how the brain works than any other kid my age, that's for sure," she said, and though she didn't sound angry, her expression revealed the opposite. "You know my dad. You think he actually cares? Since my mom has been gone, he's had no idea how to raise me." She rolled her eyes.

I would be *thrilled* if I didn't have to go to school anymore.

"So, Stasia, I was thinking I could practice some things on you," she said carefully. Every time Amelie wanted something, her voice changed into a sweet tone as if she were casting a spell on her listeners.

"Like what?" I asked, backing away from her like she was going to pull out a scalpel. I knew her too well and I wasn't going to fall prey.

"Well don't get mad…but, you know how you've always been sort of awkward?" She looked at me for agreement. I took some offense to her statement instead. "Anyway, I'd like to try age regression hypnotherapy with you."

"Age w-what?" I stammered.

She nodded confidently. "When I hypnotize you, you'll be able to return to an earlier stage of life and explore all your memories. I mean, what if aliens abducted you as a kid? What if you had some traumatic experience? Wouldn't you want to know?" Her baby blue eyes came closer to mine.

I shook my head without even hesitating.

"I've been hypnotized before by my dad," she said. "It's fun. You just feel really relaxed. Like you're a dragon."

"What did you say?" I asked, my heart pounding.

"Like you're dead. It's a figure of speech," she said slowly, meeting my eyes with hers. "Why are you so jumpy?"

There was a knock on the door and Mama walked in just as Amelie was preparing her convincing speech. Amelie looked disappointed, but I was relieved.

"Hey girls, why don't you go outside? It's going to be one of the last few days that you actually can." Mama went on autopilot, picking up all my clothes from the floor.

Amelie tried to whisper something in my ear but I pretended not to notice her attempt.

"Ok, Mama," I answered loudly, annoyed that she was always interrupting, but happy to not continue this conversation with Amelie.

By the time we were out the door, Amelie had already

forgotten about the hypnosis and was chatting to me about boys. We dragged ourselves through the snowy hill so that we could catch a close glimpse of the ocean, and maybe a quick feel. The weather let up a little and I could actually see the horizon. Clouds bunched up just where the sky met the sea and a dark orange color lingered. On the way down the hill, I could hear birds chirping and rustling in the trees. They were standing on the empty, snow-covered branches. The normal, bright colors of their feathers were muted. "Sugarbirds" I remembered was what the locals called them. With their bright yellow bellies, black heads, and petite frames, no one could resist feeding them sugar, which they went crazy for.

The mixture of ice, grass, and dirt crunched under our feet. As Amelie and I neared the beach, we passed Mr. Gordon's house, our closest neighbor. It was unusual to see his front gate open. As the gate was fully metal, with no holes to peeking eyes, I took the opportunity to size up the place. His house was at least double the size of mine and where we had ocean view, he had a beachfront. There were large boulders on each side of the beach, conveniently placed where his property line ended. I was sure he had arranged this. It had to be illegal, but no one was ever going to check. The result was that he had his own private beach, which no one could get in to unless they scaled the rocks.

Today, his driveway was clear of snow and I knew he must have spent hours shoveling the path.

"Amelie." I tapped her shoulder. "Remember Mr. Gordon?"

"Yeah, oh man, what a weirdo. Let's keep going," she said, barely glancing.

Mr. Gordon was never one for conversation. Besides the privacy he tried to create around his house, he was rarely seen outside of it. It was years before I learned that he was actually married.

I watched him sitting outside on the patio, smoking a cigar, while Amelie kept walking. He seemed so old and fragile that the cold alone could break him. He had gotten thinner since the last time I saw him five years ago. He was close to thirty-eight, Mama's age, but he looked more like fifty-five. He wore a black wool jacket with a matching scarf and hat. His eyes were large and I could see them vividly. He looked straight ahead, only moving his hand to his lips. The smoke wandered out of his mouth and rose above his head mixing in with the fog.

"Stasia! Let's go!" Amelie's voice broke the silence.

Even in the wintertime, the beach was welcoming. There was a family with two small children making snow castles and running around next to the shoreline. My mind flashed back to warmer times when we were in the exact same place, except in swimsuits and wearing sunscreen—we were two little girls running around without a care in the world.

"You have to put your hand in the water. When's the last time you touched the ocean?" Amelie asked, skipping backwards towards the sea.

The last time was on Pa's fishing boat, a few years ago at least. Every weekend we had taken the boat out to sea and had gone to neighboring islands. Mutar, St. Berri, and Antara—I remembered each one for its different qualities. Mutar had the best snorkeling, St. Berri had delicious lobster, and Antara was just deserted with the softest sand in the Caribbean. On the boat, Pa had fished and drunk beers. Just being out on the water had been the best feeling in the world. I had loved when the salt-water splashed on my face and the boat rocked over the waves. We used to jump into the ocean and swim as far as we could and music would blare from the boat speakers as we barbequed on the beach. Grilled tuna sounded very tasty right now.

"I guess three years ago," I answered, snapping back to reality. "I bet it doesn't feel the same now."

I walked closer to the calm water and bent to put my hand in. As the tips of my fingers entered, a cold sensation traveled up my arm and into the core of my body. My heart froze. Jolts of energy traveled around my midsection, ran down my legs, and finally back up into both arms until they stung in my head.

"Wow, look." Amelie motioned to the water. "Look at the colors." She was already moving around the beach, trying to peer from all angles.

Different shades of fluorescent red rippled from my fingertips, like blood being trickled through the water.

"Wow, that's amazing Stasia. What do you think that is?"

"Must be some weird effect from the sun, or the heat of my body. I don't know," I guessed.

The colors left my fingers and started to dance out into the ocean, traveling faster and faster as if they were finally let free. I removed my hand and watched as the colors kept going. When I felt something scratching my fingertips, I opened my hand to see clear scales sticking to my skin. I shook my hand quickly and they fell off, disappearing into the air.

Amelie didn't notice them. She bent down to put her hand in the water, but she yanked it out quickly, dropped her jaw and wrinkling her forehead. "Freezing!" she exclaimed.

For some reason I felt like I had to change her

attention quickly, so I laughed, picked up some snow and threw it. "Got cha!" Then I quickly ran in the other direction as fast as I could. I was scared.

AFTER I'D tossed and turned for hours, it was that night that I dreamed about Surritz for the second time. This time I seemed to be a person in this foreign land, yet everything seemed oddly familiar. I felt the cold grass under my feet, heard the call of wild animals, and smelled the dry, hot earth. My senses were heightened much more than they were in real life. As I began walking through a large field covered in dandelions, I thought of how much I missed the feeling of the warmth on my skin. It made sense that my dreams were bringing me beautiful thoughts, since nothing was beautiful about St. Michael in the rain, snow, or in the winter at all for that matter.

I walked faster and faster through the field until I was running at top speed, laughing. I was so excited to be there. My bare feet were not harmed in any way by the silky, green grass. Looking down, I could almost sense the yellow flowers' enjoyment to see me so elated. They grew taller in front of my eyes and started singing to me. All of them looked up at me and moved out of my path.

Finally, when I got to the end of the field, I lay down in the grass and it suddenly started to part as a creature approached me. A small water dragon held out a glass of water and encouraged me to drink. The water was iridescent and I knew it was from the waterfall not far away.

"Where am I?" I asked the Wayter curiously.

To my surprise, he answered, "You are here. Welcome."

Then he turned away and disappeared in the meadow.

Right as I lay back down on the ground, my eyes opened, and I saw the white ceiling in my small room. There were the red curtains. The small window. The lit candles. And the familiar mildew scent, which found its way to my nostrils.

CHAPTER 4

THE SUN went down faster than on any other day I could remember. I had been in St. Michael for five days and never noticed that I could practically watch the sun as it lowered in the sky. At 6:30 PM, I heard the little cowbell on our front gate ringing. I peered through the small window in my bedroom corner to see Amelie standing by the gate with her bright pink snowsuit on.

"Stasia, you there? I'm coming in," she yelled.

I ran downstairs to open the front door.

"Hey," she said and walked quickly past me and up to my bedroom as I followed. I closed the door behind us and sat down on the bed with her. "Remember that dream you told me about? About the foreign, beautiful, *weird* land," she asked without taking a breath.

"Yeah, why?" I replied nervously.

"I did some research. My theory is that you have had a traumatic experience as a child and are trying to cover it up with happy, beautiful dreams. I've read this stuff in the textbooks, Stasia. I know what I'm talking about."

It was true, she did read a lot, and she was obsessed

with the den, borrowing a book every time she visited. But I was sure Mama didn't stock any books about this subject.

"What could have happened?" I asked, annoyed. "I remember my whole life. It's really not that interesting."

She rested her hands in her lap before looking up again.

"If something happened, you should know. You will be so much happier. You will never feel insecure again. Just trust me. We have to do the age regression. I promise nothing will happen. If it does, we will call my father immediately. He hypnotizes people all the time."

I knew that it was only a matter of time before she mentioned the hypnosis again. I didn't like the sound of it but I knew she was giving me no choice. When Amelie got an idea in her head she never gave up until she got her way. Two parrots. $150 pair of shoes. A Jet Ski. A snowmobile. And the list goes on.

"Look Amelie, we can try it once but that's it. If it doesn't work we won't do it again," I replied firmly, positive that nothing was going to happen. I only agreed so Amelie could get her fix and we could move on. I hoped this wouldn't end up like the time she convinced me to jump off a hotel roof into the ocean. Besides almost being paralyzed, I still had pain in my lower back. Not to mention a fear of heights and nightmares of falling.

"Ok, deal," she said and we shook on it.

"How does it even work?" I asked.

"You do meditation right? It's just like...well, it's similar. Stop worrying." I saw her fiddle with something in her bag before she pulled out an old, dusty book with bent edges. She rolled her eyes when she caught my bewildered expression. "It's my father's. It's not voodoo."

I pulled the book from her hands, wanting to take a closer look. It was small but heavier than I expected. The title was in script with only a small picture of a man lying on a bed in the bottom right. It read, *A Whirlwind of Hypnosis: Self-hypnosis for the selfless*, by Alfred Piedmont.

"Believe me now?" Amelie asked, "You're like a scared little puppy."

"Look I said I'd do it," I replied but my heart pounded as I handed her the book.

"Lie down on the bed and close your eyes so I can begin," she instructed.

I lay on the bed on my back like the man on the book, rubbing my clammy hands together. Amelie got comfortable in my rocking chair and opened the book towards the end. She squinted and flipped through some more pages before she seemed content with what she was reading. She started speaking after clearing her throat loudly.

"Ok, here we go… Feel the muscles in your eyelids start to become very relaxed and very warm. Relax. Now, feel the muscles of your upper face relaxing. Relax."

I wanted to giggle at Amelie's "mature voice" but I knew she would get upset. She was taking this very seriously but I was afraid it would only put me to sleep.

"Feel the muscles around your nose and lips relax. Relax. Now, feel the muscles all around your ears and to the back of your scalp, relax. Take a deep breath and feel the warm air entering and exiting your nostrils. Breathe. Feel your belly expand."

I opened my eyes just enough to make sure she was actually reading from the book. To my surprise, she was following line by line with her fingers. My face did feel relaxed, I had to admit, and I was fighting to keep my eyelids open.

"Now, feel the muscles of your right arm relax. Feel the energy enter your nostrils and relax all the muscles of your right arm and leg."

Memories of my childhood living on St. Michael started to drift in and out of my mind. I remembered the first time I saw needlefish in the ocean. It was on a snorkeling trip to Mutar. Pa had tapped my back and I had turned around to see a large school of the fish traveling past us. Pa had been so excited to show them to me. His brown eyes had widened in his mask and he had tried to smile, which had let water into his snorkel. When he blew to get it out, the fish noticed that we were foreign moving creatures and they had swum off like shiny snakes traveling in a pack.

"Feel the muscles of your left arm, and left leg, relax. Relax your fingers. Relax your toes. Everything in your body is feeling very, very relaxed. Now, picture a bright white light entering the crown of your head and illuminating your whole body. Now, you are feeling very, very relaxed. I'm going to start counting down from five to one. When I reach one, you will have regressed back to a time as a child and you will answer all my questions."

"5..."

"4..."

"3..."

"2..."

"1... Stasia, you are a child. Tell me how old you are."

"I am seven."

"What do you see?"

"I am walking around. There is a lot of light."

"Are you outside? Tell me more about your surroundings."

"I see bright green palm trees. I hear people talking. I hear the ocean. I like the sound of the water."

"Can you tell me more?"

"I hear her pretty voice. Mama's voice. I think we are at the beach. I hear other children playing. Mama and Pa are talking. They are laughing."

"What are you feeling?"

"I feel good. I like the heat. I like to see the ocean. I want to go in the ocean. I want to swim."

"Ok, now you are leaving that time period. It's four years earlier…where are you?"

"I am three years old, lying in a room I can hardly recognize to be my own."

I could hear Amelie's breath go in and out of her mouth slowly. Her nails shuffled against her scalp.

"Tell me more." The words came crawling gently through the air until they reached my ears, which sucked them in and processed them faster than an eye could blink.

"I ask the man in the room about the dragons. Where are they? Strong jaws. Clear scales. Feather-like wings. Small. Intelligent."

"Where are you?"

I barely heard Amelie's words, as I smelled the dragon's breath in the air.

"I'm in a small bedroom. I'm screaming and a man comes in. I clearly see the expression on his face—his eyebrows squint down to his lashes, his mouth opens in horror, his nostrils flare. I can't figure out why I'm here and why he seems so concerned."

"Whose face is it?"

"The man who says he's my father. He tries to comfort me."

"Where are the dragons?"

For a moment, as I lay there, I was back in the room with Amelie. I could sense animals all around, dancing in a sort of slow motion dream state. Some were nothing but mist, but others stood on their hind legs, holding each other while they twirled and twisted, sang and smiled. Their paws stomped and slid around the floor in different rhythms that they all understood. In the distance, there was music. Once I heard it, it became so loud and powerful; I could feel it running through my bones. But then, something pulled me back, and I was back in time, in that moment again, in the small room, confused. Scared.

"The dragons are not here. But they will come. I'm frightened. This is just not me."

"Who are you then?"

"Where are the animals? Something is wrong! I'm beginning to get alarmed. I try to tell the man about what happened with the dragons. He doesn't understand. He doesn't believe me."

I heard the chair move as Amelie switched positions. I lay still, my eyes remained closed. She bent down close to me until I could smell her hair against my nose. Hot air leaked out of her mouth. A slight noise whistled through her teeth. The animals were dancing ferociously around her now. They didn't hear the noises I did. They didn't care. Their tails whipped around each other as they embraced their freedom.

"Who doesn't believe you?" she asked slowly.

I wanted to stay in the room and watch the animals that Amelie did not seem to hear. Their heads titled back as they all laughed, in animal sounds, but I understood. They were in a ballroom of their own, with their own music that played more loudly than our silence. But I was sucked back into that moment with every question that Amelie asked.

"The man that is here with me. I can't think clearly enough to figure out what's going on. I just know that it isn't right. I'm scared. I'm so scared. Please, someone help me!"

Amelie's hands were shaking so heavily that her silver bracelet clattered against the wooden nightstand. To me, the noise only blended with the beat that made the animals clap and holler, their paws intricately sliding around one another in a dance I didn't recognize, but longed to learn.

CHAPTER 5

MY ARMS were numb. I felt like I had just been through a long, refreshing sleep, the kind that takes you back to being in the womb.

"Amelie, what happened?" I asked as I began to stretch.

"Dragons?" she giggled. "Do you remember what you said?"

I remembered. But I also wanted to tell her that I sensed animals dancing around the room, sliding effortlessly between her and me, laughing, stomping, clapping, and *talking*. But surely that couldn't have been real.

"I think I was dreaming," I answered slowly.

"Clearly. You were making sense at first, but then you didn't know who you were. Oh look, it's giving me goose bumps...you want to do it again?" She flung her hair behind her shoulders and grinned happily before jumping up and down.

"No! It's a waste of time. I just fall asleep."

"You're a chicken," she said, flapping her arms like wings.

I didn't care. There was no way I was *ever* doing that again. But something resonated with me about the animals. I couldn't stop seeing their movements in my mind.

"Seriously, what if it's something?" Amelie said, her expression now serious.

Before I knew what I was saying, I blurted out, "It's just, well, you know, the dragon classes in Puncchit scared me. I've been having nightmares. I guess I just started dreaming again." I was careful to leave out the part about the footprints in the snow. *What was that about anyway?*

"People are so superstitious. I don't know how you handle it. I'm glad now that I didn't go to the classes in Puncchit."

Finally, someone was bringing me back to reality.

We both laughed. "Promise you won't tell your dad or anyone," I said. "People will think we're crazy."

The thought of people thinking I was crazy *made* me crazy. I had my own opinions, of course, but I never voiced them. Only in my head did they speak to me constantly. To the outside world, I wanted to be invisible.

"Don't worry. I won't tell a soul. The secret's safe," Amelie reassured me.

I opened the door to the smell of freshly baked apfelstrudel. I breathed in the warm scents of the freshly baked dough, spicy cinnamon, and cooked raisin. My mouth began to water, as I thought about that first bite of the crispy pastry. Mama always loved to bake. It was one of the reasons my parents were so compatible.

"Honey," she called as we headed down the creaking attic steps. I quickly gestured to Amelie again, motioning that she should not say anything to my mother. "There you girls are. Your father is on the phone, Stasia."

The rotary phone looked like an ancient artifact, but for some reason Mama liked it and thought it was a good antique. It was an ugly off-white color that was darkened on the edges from wear. I disliked even touching it, much less having to stick my fingers in the dirty holes and hold it close to my face.

I took it with two fingers. "Hey Pa."

"Stasia, you would have loved the bagels I made today on the truck. I found a way to mix in raisins, chocolate chips, cinnamon, and pistachios into the bread. What do you think we should call this one? Rachopis Bagels?"

He started telling me all about Puncchit, but I was barely interested.

"Has Maisy called Pa?"

"Oh, um, no. But how's it going there? When are you coming back to help me move out?" His voice echoed in the old device.

"Never. Having fun here with Amelie. Haven't seen her in years. Plus, I don't want Mama to be alone." I knew this would get him.

"Good idea. I think I'll come back soon, just so busy at work," he replied.

There he goes with "work." A food truck hardly qualified as work. The images "work" brought to mind were old men in suits and ties going in and out of business meetings.

"Ok talk to you soon. Bye Pa." I handed the phone back to Mama. I did want to ask him if he remembered the first time we saw the needlefish, but for some reason I hesitated.

It was getting late so we drove Amelie home. When we returned, Mama was anxious to get inside, but I stayed outside to take in the view. Tiny snowflakes fell from the clouds and landed peacefully on the branches of the palm trees. The remaining tree frogs sung, but not happily. The moon was hanging low in the sky, illuminating the ocean below it while colored sailboats swayed with the current in the bay. With the moonlight reflecting off the snow, I could see everything without any of the outdoor lamps turned on.

Slowly, snowflakes built up on my boots as I walked around, listening to the crunchy noise of the flattened snow. It was one of my favorite sounds. I could also hear my breath go in and out. My body struggled to convert the cold air into a breathable temperature. I was trembling when I suddenly noticed the same animal tracks that I had been seeing for days. They were freshly made in the snow as if the animal had been right by my side. They only went one direction, down and around the side of the house. When I followed them, I noticed that they were all the same. The same exact print over and over again. The snow laid neatly, not disturbed in the slightest. As I walked, it moved and shuffled. I hated ruining the tracks with my own.

As I turned around the corner at the back of the house, I saw something flicker in the distance. There it was. It was running. I couldn't make out the shape, but I could see that it had a tail. I followed, but the animal ran faster. Still, there was no disturbance in the snow. Could it be hopping? I ran around the house, very familiar with where each tree and lamppost stood. As I rounded the corner again at top speed, dodging Mama's garden statues and convinced I was gaining on this animal, a light suddenly turned on in the house and I could no longer see the tracks.

"Darn it!" I muttered out loud, coming to a sudden stop.

"STASIA," my name echoed.

I bolted around the third corner and down the steps to the front door. Covered in snow, I fumbled with my jacket until I saw Mama standing in the living room.

"What are you doing outside?" she asked, not amused.

"Just looking at the moon. It's full tonight," I answered innocently.

"You scared me. Come inside. It's cold. You can look at it through the window." She grabbed my arm as if I were still five years old.

THAT NIGHT, I dreamed of Surritz. From the second I fell asleep, it was like I was transported to the beautiful country. I transcended from the sky and through the ocean, until my feet touched the grass and off I went running to the nearest fruit tree. Oranges the size of soccer balls grew on these trees. When I grabbed one, I noticed how light it was. I could carry one in the palm of my hand, tossing it up and down like a balloon. Upon taking the first bite, the juice exploded in my mouth.

There were people lounging under the tree in the shade. They all wore bright clothing and were talking and laughing with each other. I tried to talk to them but they didn't respond. They couldn't see me. I started walking towards the largest tree on the hill in the distance. Dragonflies zoomed around, dodging anything in their paths. Along the way, I stopped for a drink of fresh water in the stream that ran along the trail. In it were types of fish I had never seen before with colors that left me speechless. They were all different shapes and sizes. Some looked like they were kissing, and others lay on their backs with big smiles on their faces.

As I neared the tree, the grass along the path got taller and taller until I could see nothing but the worn path itself. It was rocky and chalky, but my bare feet only felt the softness of feathers. I stopped to pick up some stones and noticed how warm they felt in my hand. They radiated heat.

"Hi there," A voice said behind me. I was relieved that someone could finally see me.

I turned around quickly to see the water dragon I had met here before. He was up on his two hind legs, smiling.

"Welcome back," he said politely.

I had seen dragons in illustrations in class, but none were as small as he was. He looked so beautiful up close. He had silky, green feathers that all lay perfectly in place. Clear scales covered his face and tail. I knew he was a Wayter because his wings looked more like fins, with gills on the top of each side, and his paws were perfectly webbed for swimming.

"What's your name?" I asked as I inspected him.

"Oh, my name is Billy. I'm so glad you decided to go to the tree on top of the hill," he said, turning to face it.

In the distance, the tree came back into view. It was a weeping willow with hundreds of leaves and too many branches to count.

"How did you know that?" I asked.

"Well this path only leads to one destination," Billy answered. He let out a long laugh, showing his thin, round purple tongue and large fangs.

"Will you come with me?" I asked, "I'd love the company."

"Yes, of course. It just so happens that I am on my way there too," he replied.

He had unusually big, caramel colored eyes and two

symmetrical horns and I couldn't believe how long his black nostrils extended. He was gorgeous, if that's possible for a dragon. He smiled at me again as if to say "thank you."

We kept walking next to each other and I got the sense that time was passing really quickly. He seemed to walk at my side for hours. I saw the landscape change from bright green to a dull brown, but Billy never changed. He had the same smile on his face and kept the same pace, walking slowly. Even when I started to run, I looked over at Billy and he was keeping the same pace, but somehow he seemed to be right by my side. I slowed down to a near crawl and Billy was still by my side, walking with the same stride.

"Are we almost there, Billy?" I asked.

"Yes, nearly," he answered excitedly.

Whenever I asked Billy a question, he looked over right away and answered as if we had been engaged in conversation the whole time.

Finally, I could smell the pine trees that surrounded the weeping willow. We were almost there. And, without so much as a parting glance at me, Billy scampered away in the grass. It bent and twisted to mold to his footsteps. *What cute paw prints*, I thought, before I awoke abruptly.

I sat up pondering this strange dream. There was something familiar, yet there was something odd. I still had the taste of the lovely orange in my mouth and the smell of the deep pine. I felt the scent travel through my body and burrow in my veins.

The funny fish in the pond still smiled at me in my mind.

And then, as if the thunder outside crashed and broke inside my head, I remembered...

Billy's paw prints were the same ones I had been

seeing in the snow all along.

CHAPTER 6

EET, EE, eet. Zip, zip. Beep. Rrrrrrip. Crickets joined the tree frog glee club center stage, for it had briefly stopped storming and the sun was shining. We could finally make it into town to stock up on some much-needed food supplies. I felt like making my own happy sounds—yeeaahh, yippee, wooot. I hadn't gone to town since I returned to the island and I was starting to go stir crazy, clearly having weird dreams and hallucinations. *Were Billy's paw prints really the ones I had been seeing in St. Michael?*

I started to think more and more about Puncchit, which upset me. Maybe it was because I wasn't having the easiest time in St. Michael since my return. I thought about Pa. I thought about the time in the water with the needlefish and how he wanted to show me something that would make me happy. And then the time on the phone the other day— he tried to include me in the decisions about pastries for BreadBar. I felt guilty about being short with him. But there were so many times he annoyed me so much. Like the time our car broke down so he drove BreadBar to pick me up outside of dragon classes, knowing quite well I was humiliated to be seen in the food truck. Or the time he probably purposely bought me pink flowered unicorn t-shirts for Christmas knowing Mama would make me wear them. I was thirteen!

So I justified reasons why I should not be feeling guilty, and I wiped the thought from my mind as the truck bounced along the uneven roads.

The center of town was bustling with activity. Baldamere's statue stared at us as if he were alive. HE WHO HATH EARS TO HEAR, LET HIM HEAR, was even bigger than the last time I remembered seeing it. Town officials had even added the painting of a Wayter flying above him.

The stores were open today for the first time in two weeks. The people I saw were much more animated than the ones at the airport. They laughed and talked loudly with one another, carrying handfuls of groceries to their cars. Crews had been around clearing the snow. I actually managed to spot a patch of green grass for the first time since I got to the island seven days ago. Everyone was cheerful and smiling, despite the temperature being only thirty-seven degrees. The sun made it feel much warmer.

"Good day!" a man on the sidewalk said as we passed by.

"How's it going?" another nodded at us.

Amelie skipped along the street in her pink jacket and green pants. She was always wearing different colors that never matched. After a brief interest in fashion she sure managed to continue her share of statements.

"You know why we are here, right?" she said, linking her arm into mine.

"For food," I said, as if it were obvious.

She leaned in closer. "We need to get figs and dates," she said, glancing at Mama from the corner of her eye.

"Why?" I asked. "And why are you whispering?"

"Because they are healthy for you."

"I like neither. Now what's the real reason?"

Carefully looking around first, she whispered again, "They're super foods that open your mind and stimulate your brain waves. How will we ever know if you really were abducted by aliens as a child?"

Amelie hadn't left me alone since the hypnosis. Every day she'd call with new foods I should eat, meditation I should practice, and even strange chanting words that she claimed would recall memories. I had to admit the hypnosis made me feel like something interesting may have happened in my life, but it wasn't something I wanted to try again. What if something terrible really did happen to me as a child? What would I do then having to live with the memories? I'd never be able to sleep again.

I laughed back at Amelie, but she stared at me blankly. She wasn't joking.

As we passed all the open stores, I smelled the fragrance from cheap air fresheners drift out of the windows. Salesmen desperate for some cash jumped out at us. They all had the same unshaven look and wore similar button-down shirts.

"My friends, come into my store, buy some canned food. Winter is here," one said.

Another extended his hand. "Just for you. I give you stereo set for fifty dollars. Half off price for you. Something to do at home through long winter."

$50 for the stereo, $60 for the batteries, I thought.

"Jackets. Three for forty dollars. Good deal. Best

price. Only today. Come inside," the third one said as the smell of liquor wandered from his mouth.

Their gapped tooth smiles didn't seem like much of an invitation. Unfortunately, there was no getting around this bartering on St. Michael.

"Check it out, Stasia." Amelie held up a striped purple and blue sweater. "How cool is this? And, only ten dollars!"

One of the snarky salesmen had scammed her into his store.

"Yeah, if you plan on never washing it," I replied a little too loudly.

"Girls, come on, we are here to buy supplies for the house. Look for food please. I don't want to drive to the supermarket on the other side of the island," Mama said.

We kept walking along the crowded sidewalk. The tree stumps of the palm trees were like old tires thrown around with no pattern as to where they stood.

"Look, Mama." I finally found a little store that was open and not crowded.

"I'm going to the store next door," said Amelie, "The one with all the incense coming out the window." She jogged along the sidewalk. "Meet me there, Stasia."

The store I entered with Mama smelled like old sardines. I looked through the shelves picking up can after can of soup, but was unsuccessful in finding any fresh food.

"I didn't know this many combinations of soup actually existed," I said, examining the labels.

"Get 'em all. We will need them," Mama chuckled.

"How much for one?" I asked the old, gray-haired man behind the register. I expected him to be excited to make a sale, but he seemed uninterested and tired.

"I give you one for one dollar," he replied slowly in

his Indian accent.

Not bad, I thought. We took thirty.

"Let's keep looking for some canned fruit," Mama said as we exited. "Go in that store and get Amelie please."

She was in a hippie store with windows that were lined with empty bottles and books. *Where are you Am?* I thought.

The store had no electricity and I fought to find my way to the back of it. Dust drifted off the shelves like it was happy to gather in the dark corners of the floor.

"Check it out!" Amelie stepped out from one of the aisles holding a game box in her hand.

"Good call. Is that Monopoly?" I asked from afar.

"No silly, look." She shoved the blue and black box in front of my face so I could clearly read the words "Ouija Board."

"I'm getting it," she said, before I could answer.

"They don't work," I warned her. "You'll be wasting money. They spell out random things, usually because someone's moving it. And if you're lucky maybe a two letter word comes every now and..."

Amelie reached in her pocket and was already paying for it before I could finish my sentence.

"It's gonna be great." She closed her eyes and motioned her hands in the air as if they were moving around a board.

"S T A S I A I S A W I T C H," she spelled out verbally.

* * *

WE GOT back home just as the crickets were starting their

nighttime songs. When I opened the front door, I was quickly greeted with a loud "Surprise!"

Pa turned around and Maisy and Flynn jumped out from behind the wooden beams. Pa's hair was messy; his t-shirt hung from his body, covering up his old, faded beach shorts. Of course he never had any *nice* shoes on and barely ever shaved. I was embarrassed, but my friends didn't seem to mind.

"We got you!" Flynn said at my astonished look.

Flynn and I quickly became friends after he had told my class in Puncchit about his summer fishing excursions with his dad. We had talked for days about the Great White shark his dad had spent hours reeling in. He had always been interested in the fishermen's life and I'd had plenty of stories from St. Michael.

I looked at Mama thinking she wouldn't be okay with this, but to my surprise she was grinning.

"Mama, you knew about this?" I asked as Amelie laughed as well. "*All* of you guys knew?"

"Your friends wanted to see you. Plus there's no school in Puncchit anyway," Mama said. "Might as well have everyone here. It *has* been really lonely cooped up in this house."

Maisy and Flynn hugged me so hard like they believed I *had* actually been starving in the Caribbean. Ironically, it was now a possibility.

"So, this is the mysterious island you're from," said Flynn. "I thought you were making it up the whole time!"

"I'm glad you came. It's been interesting here to say the least," I replied.

I introduced Amelie to my two, and only, Puncchit friends. Maisy and Amelie had similar thin bodies, but Maisy's red hair set her apart.

"Yeah, actually, I've known for a while that your friends were visiting," Amelie boasted.

"Really?" I asked.

Amelie grabbed my hand and whispered in my ear. "Why do you think I got the Ouija Board?" She winked. "Because now we will have players."

THAT NIGHT, it was three against one and I was forced to participate in the game. My dark attic room was transformed into a séance session. Amelie lit candles and pulled out the incense and strange smelling oils she had purchased in town without me noticing. I had made her promise not to tell Maisy and Flynn about the hypnosis, and that if we used the Ouija board it would just be for fun.

"So this is what you guys do for fun?" Flynn asked, taking the words right from my mind.

"Well, we used to go to the beach and snorkel, and do all the things you dream of doing on vacation. I wish you could have come in the summer. It's not usually like this," I replied quickly, embarrassed. *What is he going to think of me now?* The St. Michael stories I'd told never consisted of ghosts.

Amelie was so busy placing candles around the windows that she didn't even acknowledge that Flynn was speaking. We cracked open one of the wooden louvers to let some cold air in. According to Amelie, spirits couldn't be attracted if it was warm.

"Have you done this before?" Maisy asked me.

I started to explain again that we don't usually play board games but she interrupted by saying, "It's gonna be fun. I'm excited!"

We all shivered as we put our fingers on the

planchette and Amelie decided she would be the medium and began the questioning.

"I'm announcing that this session will only allow a positive experience to take place. No negative forces or energy is allowed in."

She sounded like she had done this before. Flynn and Maisy looked at me for answers. I shrugged.

"Is there an entity in the room?" Amelie continued.

We all waited. Nothing happened.

She repeated, "Is there an entity in the room?"

"Is there an entity in the room?" Flynn mimicked quietly.

Maisy giggled but Amelie remained silent. The pointer moved slightly. Amelie kept her eyes closed.

"Can you hear me?" she asked, stressing each word slowly.

The pointer started to move down before coming back up. We weren't convinced.

"Is there an entity in the room?" Amelie asked for the third time, opening her eyes just as the pointer moved swiftly to the bottom right hand corner. It stopped over the Y.

My heart started to beat faster.

Maisy's eyes opened and her lips pressed together.

Flynn remained cool. I wondered if he had moved the pointer. He wasn't taking this seriously, after all.

"Who are you here to see?" Amelie asked, again closing her eyes.

The pointer did not move.

She asked the question again.

Still, there was no activity.

The four of us sat like statues. Out of the corner of my eye, I watched as the candlelight flickered in the wind.

The moonlight illuminated enough of the room to cast a white, silvery glow. I was so cold that my fingers started to go numb. I could feel my nose running.

"Ask another yes or no question," Maisy whispered.

"Are you here to see Stasia?" Amelie asked confidently.

The pointer started to move rapidly, first in a circle, before moving down, and finally back up. All of our bodies moved in unison as we tried to keep our fingers planted on the pointer. It spun around until it ended up right on the "Y" again.

I looked at Flynn, directly now, convinced that he was moving the pointer. He looked down, his expression unchanging. How could anyone remain calm in this situation?

"Can you tell us why you are here?" Amelie asked in an unfamiliar deep voice.

Nothing happened.

"Where are you from?"

Again, there was no movement.

Maisy's face was pale and her mouth remained slightly open as she breathed in and out deeply. She did not move her eyes off the board.

Amelie, however, seemed calm. She was the only one who knew what she was doing. She had specifically put on her Indian inspired muumuu robe, wore her hair in braids, and had tied a scarf around her forehead. A pink scarf, nonetheless.

I was sure all of them were playing a trick on me, Maisy being a better actor than Flynn.

"Ok, this is silly," I whispered. "Who's moving the pointer? Not funny Amelie, come on. You're freaking me out."

All three looked at me and no one said anything.

"Stasia, we are trying to contact an entity. You must believe in it or else it won't work. Let's ask another question," Amelie said after a few moments.

"Let's at least close the window, I'm freezing," I replied back softly.

"Ok, just one more question," she answered. "And then we'll stop… for now."

She closed her eyes and spoke sternly. "What is your name?"

I watched the pointer carefully. It didn't move.

We sat together, quietly. Contemplating how long I should play along before getting up, I started to count down from twenty. When I reached one, I was going to quit playing, turn on the lights, and call it a night.

When I sounded out four in my mind, the pointer started to jerk. It went quickly to the top left hand corner and hovered around slightly until it slowly slid over the "B".

Then, it jolted to the right, then back to the left, before moving slowly to the right again and stopping completely over the "I".

It moved more again to the right, jolted around and then stopped on the "L".

I started seeing double. I was getting shortness of breath. I began to sweat even though I couldn't feel my frozen hands. Was my imagination moving the pointer? It lingered over the "L" and seemed to be vibrating, incapable of moving. Then, in less than a second, it shot down to the "Y".

We kept our fingers on the pointer for another few minutes. There was no more movement. It was done.

"Bily," Maisy said. "It spelled out Bily."

"Does anyone know a Bily?" Amelie asked.

"That's not even a name," Flynn scoffed.

All three looked at me for a possible connection.

I shook my head in disbelief. "Billy. It spelled out Billy."

CHAPTER 7

THE COLD sand spilled out of my hands through my fingers. Every little particle fought to get back on the beach where it belonged. The small amount that remained in the middle of my palm was white and soft. There were no shell particles. I loved the beaches on St. Michael for that reason. They all stretched for miles and miles with no garbage or any trace of humanity. As I thought about the revelations the Ouija board provided last night, I extended my hand into the icy ocean. Humming a melody, I drew clouds with my fingers in the water. I imagined it being still and warm; my thoughts brought nostalgia for my younger days.

The ocean was as calm as a turtle in the sun. I stared into the transparent sea, reminiscing about my childhood until the water slowly started to rock, then jerk back and forth as if electricity had hit it. It started to blur and a gray color appeared. Soon, colors started emerging from the gray. Staring in a sort of trance, I saw moving memories of my childhood in the water. It was as if I was watching a TV program of my home videos.

My first day of school flashed by. I was seven. I

watched as Mama brushed my hair and put it back in a ponytail.

"Ready for school, Stasia Bear?" she had asked, smiling and holding my hand.

"Yeah!" my small self had screamed back. My pink blouse had been tucked into my denim skirt. Around my shoulder, I had worn a yellow purse instead of a backpack. I'd forgotten all about that purse!

In the memory that was shown to me, I was looking down at my sequined flip-flops. Those were the days of warmer weather. I'd hopped out of Mama's vanity seat and onto the bed. My pink nail polish had been chipped at the time and I had been wearing plastic neon rings on each finger.

"We have to get going," Mama had said. "We have to pick up Amelie on the way."

Bright colored beach toys had been scattered around the yard and round, yellow mangoes had been hanging from the trees, begging to be picked. Scents of jasmine were filling our noses.

The entire yard had been bustling with green foliage and colored flowers. Mama had grabbed a red hibiscus and had stuffed it over my ear.

As a child, I had taken everything for granted. Tourists had constantly asked, "What's it like to live in paradise?" But I'd never understood what they had meant. Now, I saw my childhood in a whole different light.

I felt as though I'd gone back in time. As I watched the scenes from my childhood, I could also feel, smell, and hear things as if they were actually there. I forgot all about how cold and dreary it was. I was sitting on an empty beach in the winter, with my hands in freezing water, but all I felt was the sunshine on my face and the smells of fresh fruit under my nose.

In the scene, we had stopped in front of Dr. Rose's house, and I quickly noticed Amelie standing with her mother outside. Tears welled in my eyes as I saw how pretty and lively Amelie's mother once was. She had been tall and slender, with long golden blonde hair and the same blue eyes that Amelie had. We had never imagined that three years later she would've been gone. She had given Amelie a small kiss on the forehead and Amelie had jumped into the back of our Volkswagen.

"Have fun dear," she had said to Amelie in her French accent.

The two of us waved goodbye and she blew Amelie one more kiss through the air. "Au revoir."

I could now feel the love she'd had for her daughter. It was the same love Mama had for me.

"I don't want to go to school," Amelie had said to me. Her big, sad eyes stared into mine. "Remember last weekend we went out on the boat with your daddy, and there was a big tunnel going from the clouds to the bottom of the ocean? I want to be there," little Amelie had said.

I snapped out of the memory and felt the cold winter breeze brush against my skin. I had completely forgotten about that boat trip. But, as I began visualizing it in my mind, the pictures started to reappear in the water. They started to move, faster and faster until they blended together again.

Out in the middle of the ocean, there had been a storm that consisted of only one dark rain cloud threatening to soak us. But instead, a large waterspout had developed, dipping closer and closer into the sea. It was so close to the boat that Pa had run to turn on the engines in the hopes of speeding away. Amelie had gone into the cabin to grab a camera, but I had stretched out my hand hoping that the waterspout would come closer so I could touch it. It was something I'd never seen before and haven't seen since. Whenever Pa had told this story, people said that when a waterspout touches the ocean, it roars around like a tornado before disintegrating. I distinctly remember this one opening up the ocean like a deep, dark hole—I'd stared down into the underworld. I just can't remember what I had seen. And why wasn't this flashback on the water showing it to me now?

As those memories faded, I saw myself in the car again. I had looked back at baby Amelie and replied, "It was scary. I want to go to school."

She had frowned, and the scene started to fade away. Ripples and colors came off my fingers and the images disappeared.

I suddenly started to shiver. There were only big, brown bushes where colorful flowers used to be, and they were covered in snow. I was alone again and I longed for my memories.

* * *

AMELIE WAS waiting for me in the kitchen when I got back home. She had let herself in and was eating Mama's aloo pie. It smelled so good it made my stomach call for it. I didn't realize how hungry I was.

"Anymore dreams of Billy?" she asked.

"No, you didn't tell Maisy and Flynn right?" I replied nervously. Really nervously. I almost regretted telling her who Billy was.

"No, I haven't seen them today. They're napping.

They don't know anything except that stupid board spelled out Billy. Besides, Flynn told me he thought you were moving it anyway," she moaned.

Why did that bother me? Maybe because I wished he trusted me more, but clearly he felt more comfortable confiding in Amelie. I cut off a piece of the pie as my mouth watered for it.

"Do you remember when we were little, out on my dad's boat, and we saw a waterspout?"

Her eyes squinted. "Yeah, of course I remember. Remember that funnel? I haven't thought about that since!"

"Do you think it was symbolic of something?" I asked carefully.

"Yeah, maybe you're a water dragon. Your mind is always working, wondering, wandering. Does it get tiring?" She was stuffing the fried potato dough in her mouth, barely paying attention to me.

"Every time I go near the ocean strange things happen. Remember the other day we saw all those red colors when I put my hand in the water?"

"That could be anything, Stasia. You're overthinking it." She stopped eating to pull her hair back into a tight bun.

"You're the one who believes in spirits," I snapped back. "Besides, ever since you hypnotized me, I have been seeing scenes of my childhood. Like all of a sudden I can remember things."

"Like what?" She finally seemed half-interested and was looking directly at me now, as if I were a specimen.

"Well, I just think about things and I can remember them better, that's all." I tried to make it seem normal. "For instance, the waterspout. It just came to me when I went to the beach. I hadn't thought of it since the year it happened."

She nodded at me like she sympathized before she pulled out some M&M's from her back pocket and began popping the little chocolates in her mouth one by one.

"You do know what that means right?" she said casually, counting the candy as they fell into her palm. "I mean, it only points to one thing."

"What?" I asked curiously before her head shot up and she stopped chewing.

"Well… It means we have to do the hypnosis again. It's the only way we will find out what's going on in that brain," she said, as she knocked her fist lightly against my forehead.

That night, Mama's red lips opened wide as she laughed so hard her whole body shook. I watched from behind the glass door as Mama and Pa sat on the porch. Their mouths moved and lips pursed, hands flew, and heads shook. It was like a silent film that I couldn't look away from. Their big coats made them look like two love struck penguins. Pa had a clean-shaven beard, finally, and a button down red and white shirt underneath his puffy jacket.

Watching them together should have made me feel happy, but it made me feel lonely instead. I immediately thought of Amelie who was confident and charismatic.

"Theater's open. You wanna go?" Maisy interrupted my thoughts as she walked out of the guest room. She and Flynn were already dressed.

"Your mom and dad want to go," Flynn added.

"Annoying," I mumbled.

He walked a little closer to my ear, speaking with his mouth half-closed. "It's okay Stasia. They're cool."

But I was referring to him. What was he doing here anyway? He came down to the island supposedly wanting to hang out with me, but all he was doing was spending time with Maisy and Amelie. He hadn't even bothered asking me if I was okay, or where I was this morning. He didn't seem interested in what was going on, and not once had he asked who Billy was.

"You going?" I asked Amelie, ignoring Flynn.

"No," she replied, winking at me.

I fought with myself on whether I should just enjoy my friends instead of giving in to Amelie's nonsense. I wanted to spend time with them, but I was now too interested in the hypnosis to stop.

"Guess I'll stay with Amelie. You guys go ahead." I sighed.

Flynn gave me a sympathetic sigh, looking at my parents and then shrugging. I rolled my eyes to play along.

The truth was that I was getting sucked into Amelie's plans. Secretly, I had begun to think more and more about the answers hypnosis could provide.

"You're missing out!" Maisy frowned before walking onto the porch to greet my parents.

"Bye Mama, bye Pa. See you later!" I said.

They turned around and waved to me through the window.

Amelie and I marched into the attic like we were going to war. I lay down on the bed in the same fashion I had before, even before Amelie had to ask me to. I was somewhat terrified, but more curious.

"So, you're liking this now?" Amelie chuckled.

I turned my head the other way. "Not exactly."

"It's not a bad thing, you know. Like I said, I have done it too."

"Ok, let's just get started. If anything weird starts to

happen, just wake me."

"Yeah, yeah, don't worry so much. All safe. All good."
She loosened her clothing before grabbing the book.

"Now, you are completely relaxed. Every muscle in your body feels relaxed. You are surrounded by a bright white light and safeguarded from anything that may endanger you. I'm going to count back from five to one. You will remember everything I ask you, but you will not feel the bad emotions that come with those experiences."

She went on and on but I tried to focus only on each of my muscles relaxing. Did I want to do this because of the information I'd find out or because the feeling was so good? Was it like an addiction I just couldn't get enough of?

"5…"

"4…"

"3…"

"2…"

"1…You are thirteen years old. What do you see?"

"I am holding my aunt's hand and we are walking through a large field. I look up at the sky; it's very blue. I'm feeling happy. I don't have any worries. I can see my hair past my shoulders."

"Who else is there with you? What are they saying? Can you hear conversations?"

"People are talking all around me. I think we are at a picnic. I can smell the fresh air and I feel the sunshine. It is very bright."

"What are you doing there?"

"We are here to celebrate a birthday. I hear everyone saying happy birthday. There's beautiful music. Now I hear my aunt talk to me. "Nina, say happy birthday to Uncle Pete.""

I see my uncle. He smiles at me. He's very happy to see me."

"Why does your aunt call you Nina?"

"That's my name. My uncle gives me a big hug."

"Are you in St. Michael?"

"No. It is different. There are no cars around. I can see fields and water. I can smell many different scents in the air. I can see many colors. Colors I can't explain."

"Ten years has passed since that day. Where are you now?"

"I'm twenty-three. I'm running through tunnels. I'm very scared. Something is happening. It's dark. I'm having trouble seeing, except, I see dark eyes. He is headed my way. I know he is coming to get me. I hear only my footsteps as I run."

"You are safe. Tell me what happened."

"He's very angry. He wants to take over Surritz. As he nears, his thoughts penetrate my mind. Anger. Hate."

"What is he mad about?"

"There is no escaping. He grabs me, something hits me, and I feel myself dying. There is pain and then, faster than I can comprehend what has happened, I am gone."

CHAPTER 8

AMELIE'S EYES lit up like the first time we plug in the Christmas tree lights each year.

"You fell asleep!" she exclaimed. "The next time we do hypnosis you need to be sitting upright."

She was interested this time. And I remembered everything I'd said. It seemed real. Too real.

"I have been dreaming about this place, Surritz. I must have fallen asleep and started talking to you about it."

I looked to Amelie for reassurance, but she had no comforting answers to provide. She wasn't looking for answers; she was looking for excitement.

"It was fascinating. When you were talking, your facial expressions were changing. In the happy moments you would smile and look like you were missing something that was great. Then, when you started describing how you died, your eyes cringed and your mouth opened as if you were going to scream," Amelie said excitedly, "Is this the place that you keep dreaming about where you talk to Billy?"

"Yes!" I exclaimed. "I have never had dreams that I can remember so vividly. It's so weird Amelie. What if something really strange is going on? I mean, lately I have been feeling like I really don't belong here."

"Belong where?" she asked.

"Here. In St. Michael. Puncchit. It just doesn't feel right."

"I think you've just explained how every teenager in the world feels. Stop thinking so much. Your imagination is running wild. You should write a book."

Outside, the moon was hanging low in the sky. The wind was jumping from tree to tree as the frogs fought to sing a little louder. The only things I saw in St. Michael lately were the moon, the ocean, and snow.

"This weather must be making me depressed," I sighed.

As Amelie drifted off to sleep on my bed, I lay awake next to her. "Nina," I whispered out loud, hoping something would ring a bell. But nothing came to me. In fact, nothing was familiar about that name at all. It was as if I'd never heard it before.

It was 11PM when a noise outside jolted me out of my thoughts. The cowbell croaked out a sleepy ring as the front gate opened. I peered out of my oval shaped window to see Mama and Pa followed by Maisy and Flynn walking through the snow. Amelie woke and grumbled something before joining me as I rushed downstairs to greet them.

"You missed a great movie!" Flynn interrupted as he dashed through the front door a few minutes later. Maisy, Mama, and Pa all followed nodding. "And, it was packed! Who knew so many people actually lived on St. Michael."

"It's so different from Puncchit here. I had never been to the Caribbean before, but I never imagined it like this," said Maisy.

They all had pink faces and were bundled up in coats, scarves, and hats.

"I never imagined I'd see my parents wear those outfits in St. Michael!" I laughed.

We all talked a little bit about how cold it'd gotten in the Caribbean. I shared the news story about the anchors making fun of the climate experts. Pa revealed that he's not happy about having to wear socks and sweaters. God forbid the mittens.

"Well I do agree that the snow is much more fun here than in Puncchit," Maisy said, stripping off her outerwear.

"Agreed," I added, "because who wants to deal with it getting all brown and slushy from the dirt and pollution."

We both crinkled our lips and noses.

"But at least they do clear the streets there," Maisy said.

"But if they did here, we would have never seen those footprints," said Flynn.

Footprints?

"Where?" I asked, more alert than ever.

"Coming from up the road, to the front door. Fresh in the snow. Looks like some sort of cat," Maisy explained.

"We've been seeing a lot of those lately, haven't we Stasia? My bet's on the iguanas. Cats don't have long toes like that," Mama said, completely unaware that I was on the lookout for a water dragon named Billy.

"Amelie, let's check it out." I barely looked at her before I started walking to the front door.

I'm not crazy, I kept repeating in my mind. *Tonight is the night I will talk to you on Earth, Billy.*

"No thanks, crazy woman. It's freezing. You're insane. I'm not going to hunt down a wild reptile. You know

68

if they are hungry enough, they will bite your hand off and eat it." Her voice trailed off as I opened the front door. The cold wind stung my eyes.

"Be right back," I called to them from the distance, but I wasn't coming back. Not until I found Billy.

"Bundle up, Stasia, please," Mama shouted after me.

As I looked back at them, they looked like little puppets in a dollhouse. Their jaws moved as they talked, hands raised up and down, smiles spread quickly. Each of their bodies bobbed from side to side as they walked in unison towards the living room. None of them had any idea what was going on inside my head. *Why was I the one this was happening to?*

I followed the footprints through our yard, weaving in and out of bushes. The tracks went through the back gate and down the road. I was so mesmerized by the prints that by the time I looked up, I had no idea where I had walked. I was in the middle of the woods when I spotted a red glow in front of me. It got bigger and brighter as I approached it through the fog. Then, it took off. I raced down the snowy slope trying to keep up with Billy. Certain parts of his body came into view, and then disappeared. I tried to follow the footprints I knew so well. If I lost sight of him, I knew it would be a long time before I'd be able to see him again. Thankfully, the moon was in clear view and made the prints easier to see in the dark night.

Thousands of stars dotted the night's sky. Twigs rustled underneath the snow as my feet hit them running. The small path Billy was taking through the woods was barely big enough for me to fit through and I had to squeeze between barren tree branches and bushes to keep him in sight. *Keep going*, I thought. *Just keep going.*

I breathed as hard as I ran fast. My gloveless hands started to tingle and sting from the night's chill. We seemed to be running for hours. I knew St. Michael like the back of my hand, but in the dark woods I could not figure out where we were going. Snow fell off the branches as I brushed by and I fought to follow his footprints in front of me. *I can't give up now*, I thought.

I still saw Billy's outline in the distance. I only knew that he was there because a bright red color radiated from his tail. I struggled to keep up as he rounded corners and ducked under trees. *Why was he running so fast?*

Finally, when I started to get closer and closer to him, I saw the trees open up to a beautiful, private beach. There he stood, in clear view now, looking out at the ocean waves. It was the first time I saw Billy's whole body in reality. He looked just as he did in my dreams—a small, green dragon with small wings and a long tail with scales. The moon illuminated the whole beach in front of us; the smell of sticky salt wandered to my nostrils and I breathed in heavily. The sand was smooth like baking powder, and to my surprise, it was warm. I spread some on my arms like bath soap.

"Go ahead. Take off your coat," Billy instructed. "You don't want it to get wet do you?"

I slipped my coat off and the warm, dewy air clung to my skin.

"Where are we?" I asked Billy, amazed at how warm it was.

"Well on St. Michael of course. You only traveled a half mile through the woods," he chuckled.

When I finally registered what he was saying, I immediately asked what he meant by "get wet".

"Well, my dear, straight below us is Surritz. This is the

only point on Earth where the warm weather filters upward and changes the whole atmospheric temperature. It never gets cold here, not with these around." He opened his paws to reveal small colored gems. "But, remember, only when you hold the gems can you feel the warmth."

What would the weather experts have to say about that? I thought.

"I slipped one in your pocket earlier, at the house. That way you could follow me here and experience this." He motioned to the whole scene, and I knew what he meant. The tropical paradise could never naturally occur on St. Michael right now. "Here." Billy picked up some sand. "If you look close enough, you can find them too."

He dug through the sand with his two front paws like a dog in the dirt.

"Here's another one!" he yelled, looking pleased.

He held his paw to my face so I could take a closer look. A sparkly, very small, uneven-sided pebble lay in his hand. I was so amazed that there was a talking animal in front of me that I could barely speak.

"Is this a diamond?" I asked the dragon I had just spent three months learning about in Puncchit.

"Yes. Isn't it beautiful? But this is the only stone that doesn't have any *useful* powers."

"Powers?" I asked, but he ignored me.

"Here, take a look at this one." A fluorescent, green emerald laid in his other paw. "This one heals."

He tucked my hand around the gem. "Close your eyes. Can you feel it?"

I shook my head slowly, automatically.

"The healing energy," he clarified.

Now, something started happening. It felt like

earthworms were traveling in circles around my elbow before burrowing themselves into my skin—an itchy but soothing sensation that happened simultaneously.

I threw my left hand onto that arm and rubbed up and down to make sure no animal had taken residence. My scraped, bleeding elbow from the run down to the beach was no longer throbbing. My cut had already scabbed over.

"Where do they come from?" I asked Billy.

"They are made from our largest rock volcano called Blootea; it extends just above Surritz into the bottom of the ocean floor. The waves carve these magnificent gems when they get spit out. Usually they fall into our waterfall where we can collect them. But, other times, they get sucked into an ocean funnel that shoots them out here." He chuckled. "I believe we should get going. Come on now." He jumped right into the ocean.

"You're a Wayter," I finally managed to say.

"Of course I am," he replied.

The water started to move around him. I had no idea what we were doing and why I believed I could follow a water dragon into the sea at night. But something about it felt right.

"Am I dreaming?" I yelled to Billy as he swirled around.

"Waaaaiiiit," he hollered. "Youuu muuuuust steeep on thaaat rooock." He pointed to a dark, circular rock next to the shore. "To signal the cloooouds."

He continued to swirl, now much faster than before.

"It's the doooown button!" His words echoed just above the wind.

I stepped on the rock and leaped in the water, expecting again that it would be freezing, but it was more than inviting—it was invigorating. The water shook around me as two large waterspouts started forming in the sky.

"See you on the flipsiiiide," Billy wailed as the spout came closer and closer to my head. Crashing waves finally drowned out his words completely.

"Wait!" I yelled panicking as I looked at the dark ocean that went on for miles.

As the spout made contact, my legs got sucked in first and then I felt like I was traveling through a tunnel. Faster and faster I zoomed downward. I could swim so fast in the water that I was able to move around more quickly than I had ever done before. I felt like I was in a warm cocoon. As I went farther and farther downwards, the colors started to change. What I thought was a beautiful bright blue ocean in St. Michael was dull compared to the colors I was seeing now.

When I finally got a grip on what was happening, I noticed all the sea life I'd been passing in the funnel. They hardly seemed to notice what was happening to me. An irritated, sleepy shark opened his eyes slowly, wondering what I was doing down there. A seahorse bobbed around scared by my presence, as he had never seen a human before. I realized that I could feel what they were feeling. I could hear what they were thinking! They stayed put throughout my whole adventure downwards. I wondered if they lived in the ocean or were permanently living in this funnel.

Suddenly, I knew the answer as if it were pulled out of thin air! They were here to answer any questions I had.

I looked at the seahorse and thought, *where are we going?*

I was instantly given an answer by a needlefish that seemed to recognize me. *To Surritz of course. We will be so glad to have you back. We have missed you, you know.*

In a second, the seahorse, shark, and needlefish were gone. I watched them float up along with the water and I was heading towards land. As I looked down, I could see the bright colors of flowers and trees. I could smell the fruit. No, I could *taste* the fruit! How delicious!

Downward I went, closer and closer to land, until the funnel curved around and I stepped right out of the ocean like I'd been on a water slide. Billy slid out right next to me.

"You know, I've had to swim that when I missed the spout. Let me tell you it takes a lot longer than four seconds," he said.

"Four seconds!" I gasped, "I felt like I was in there for hours!"

His large eyes squinted as his closed lips shifted and he began to shake his head. "Time is not a linear existence. Time has so many dimensions, it always confuses me when I am…up there," Billy explained. "Well, look around. Feel familiar?"

It did feel familiar. Too familiar. There were the trees, the flowers, the fruit, and the colors. Everything I'd seen in my dreams was right here in front of my face, except, no one was around.

"Yes, I've been dreaming of this place. What is it?"

"Not only dreaming of it." He laughed. "All in due time."

The ocean surrounded us on all sides like a bubble of life under the sea.

"The reason no one on Earth can get to the bottom of the sea, or learn much about it is because the sea connects all the different realms together. There are many different worlds that share the same waters. In Surritz, the water respects the boundaries of our country. Every single thing, including the ocean is alive and has a conscience." He continued, "If it wanted to, the ocean could flood all of Surritz and we would all diminish. It chooses not to."

Above our heads, the waves crashed back into themselves without falling.

Just like in my dreams, Surritz was the most beautiful place I'd ever seen. I wasn't looking at things that had color; I was looking at colors that were made up of things!

"Let's talk about your dreams," Billy interrupted my thoughts. "I've been trying to make myself visible, but it's just so hard in your world."

"What do you mean?" I asked.

"I always walk right up to you, wave my paws and wings like a *wild* animal, but all you ever see are my footprints. You start to follow them, when in reality, I'm standing right next to you!" he said.

That explained it. "No wonder your tracks were always so fresh, but I could never find you!"

"Didn't you see my color?" he asked.

"Color?"

"People on Earth are brilliant. They have learned to mask colored energy with objects! It's astounding. Just genius!" he said before continuing, "It was easier for me to send you information in your dreams. In that state, your mind was open to the suggestions. Have you figured out what is going on yet? You knew as a child, but then something happened and your memories were erased."

I wanted to know what he was talking about, but I didn't. I just couldn't...I couldn't remember.

"Relax. Think," he said, opening his paws slowly and taking a deep breath.

I closed my eyes and could smell freshly cut flowers

and new budding fruit as if they were right under my nose. Images flashed through my mind. I saw pictures of myself. My hair. My arms. My feet. But, that wasn't me. It was Nina, the girl I saw in the hypnosis. Was that me?

"I lived here once?" I asked Billy. "Yes, I was killed. How long ago was that? How long has it been?"

Billy nodded, "Well, not that long actually. Fifteen years, three months, five days, ten hours, seven minutes, and two seconds to be exact. When you died, you immediately reincarnated to Earth. We were all hoping you'd come back to Surritz so we could find you more easily," Billy answered.

"Find me for what?"

"Oh, that's a conversation for another time. Let's get situated!"

I looked around at the quiet, peaceful area. Fish swam by, grass blew in the wind, and smoke rose from little chimneys creating different designs in the air. I recognized one to be a horse; the other was a zebra. A goat, a cow, an elephant. They *all* started to make animal shapes. The smoke blew my way quickly before I found myself swatting the animals away from my face.

"This place looks perfectly fine," I said, "What could you possibly need from an average girl like me?"

"Not my place to say. Abe Carlton might read your thoughts at the wrong time if I told you. He might be able to transcend the ocean, just as I did to find you. You don't want him to kill you again...do you?"

"Who is Abe?" I asked.

But Billy just squeezed my hand before he left me in the middle of the island alone. I took my index finger and thumb and pinched my skin as hard as I could. *Am I still sleeping?*

Part of me wanted to run in the grass and tumble and roll like a little child would. But, a bigger part of me wanted to go home. I thought of Mama and Pa who were probably going crazy wondering where I was. In my mind, the images of them being happy puppets changed quickly to them being prisoners in an insane asylum running in all directions, screaming and ripping their hair out. I didn't know how much time had passed but it had to be hours. It would surely be the middle of the night once I returned.

How do I get back? I panicked looking around for Billy, or for anyone who could direct me. I didn't see a speck of life anywhere.

But just after I thought it, the words came flowing through my mind. I read them like moving words on a scroll: *Back the way you came. Yes, right over there.*

I neared the edge of the water. Looking at it, I watched some angelfish swim by. It was like looking at a huge aquarium yet there was no glass. I put my right foot through and watched as the water conformed around my ankle. My right arm went next, and I slowly inched towards the water until half my body was in the ocean. With my right eye, I saw many more creatures swim by; there was tuna, clown fish, turtles and dolphins! All seemed confused, wondering what I was doing. Some of them thought I was crazy and purposely swam by very quickly. Others laughed at my ignorance. As I tugged the left side of my body into the water, I felt the pull of the ocean. It sucked me in and I started to spin. *Here we go*, I thought, before I shot up like a missile.

WHEN I got back to the beach in St. Michael, I lay on the warm sand to dry off, for in the distance I saw the snowcapped trees and barren land. On the other side of the imaginary line, it was snowing! I piled my hair on top of my head and picked up the jacket I'd left on the beach.

As I made my way into the forest, the warm beach began to disappear. It started to get very cold again. I could feel my hair freezing and my head pounding.

When I neared the house, I heard Mama laughing from behind the closed door. She had one of those laughs that could not be mistaken for anyone else's. It was inverted. While most people laughed by letting out sound and air, Mama sucked in air, while trying to make sounds at the same time. It always came across like a mix between someone choking while trying to sing. While I always made fun of her for this, tonight I was so happy to hear it.

I opened the door slowly and saw everyone sitting around the living room table, talking as if they hadn't been worried about me being gone so long.

"It was exactly four hundred and eighty-seven pounds. A big one!" Pa said to Flynn and I already knew what he was talking about. How could I not? It was about the biggest marlin he'd ever caught; I had probably heard the story about fifty times.

When they noticed me, they all turned around casually.

"Did you find it?" Mama said to me, still smiling at Flynn's response.

"What?" I asked.

"The animal. I guess you hardly looked. Too cold?" She chuckled.

I glanced at the clock in the living room and noticed that only minutes had elapsed since I'd left. I felt the confused, blank expression develop on my face. *I SAW A WAYTER!* It was the only thing I could scream in my head.

What would Pa say if I told him? Would he believe me? Would the town drag me to a firing squad death for my lies? Or would they praise me like Baldamere?

"Are you okay?" Mama asked, concerned now.

"I'm just cold. I'm going to go dry off," I said, almost in tears.

"So, did you find out what it was, Stasia?" Amelie asked with a sarcastic tone.

"We should all be heading to bed. I'm exhausted," Pa said to Mama.

Before I turned around, I noticed all the familiar faces—Amelie was twirling her hair, Flynn was talking to Maisy, Mama was looking at me worried, and Pa was drinking the last of his red wine—but I couldn't stop thinking about Billy and where I'd been.

The TV was on mute as I lay in bed that night, trying to fall asleep to the happy images of Lucy and Ethel trying to work in a chocolate factory. But my mind was in a different place as I tried desperately to remember the life I once lived. *My past life.* I kept repeating the words in my head. I never thought about past lives before. Did we all have them?

"Knock, knock," Mama's voice called from behind my bedroom door, but she was already opening it. "What's wrong? Why did you look so worried?" she asked.

The conflicting sides of my brain fought with each other again. The right side was apprehensive and wanted to ask Mama what was going on. The left side told me there was a logical reason behind all of this. *Stay calm,* it directed.

I decided that now was as good a time as any to ask.

"Mama, what was I like as a child?" I didn't expect an answer anything less than "charming," "sweet," or "cute." I asked anyway. I needed to know the truth.

"As darling as ever," she replied quickly, too quickly for it to be genuine. But a huge smile spread across her face and that comforted me.

"No, really. Was I different?"

Of course I was different. Tall. Quiet. Confused. Shy. *That was not the most efficient way to ask the question*, my left-brain informed me.

Mama just smirked, avoiding the question. I got the nervous, anxious pains that stabbed my sides and made my stomach turn. She didn't have to speak for me to know that she was hiding something. My relationship with her could almost exist without any words—I could tell what every little movement of her body meant.

"Did Amelie say something to you?"

"No, why? What does Amelie know?" I pressed.

"You were...reserved, that's all. Dr. Rose helped you come out of your shell a little bit." She massaged my arms with her thumbs, running her fingers through mine as if to say that the conversation had concluded.

"What are you talking about? You never told me what happened. Tell me Mama!" I begged.

She took her hands away from mine and started playing with her rings, twirling them around as she always did when she was either worried or distressed.

"You seemed scared as a child, which we could never really figure out. When you were old enough to talk, you said you didn't want to be here."

"Where? In St. Michael?"

"We didn't know what you were talking about. You always wanted to be alone. You said this wasn't your life. That you belonged elsewhere. You spoke of strange things, frequently. One day, you were telling stories of animals and dragons. You were only three years old, but the descriptions you were giving were so detailed. It was unbelievable."

I pleaded with her to tell me what happened that day, but she was still too hesitant.

"Why are you so interested? Is someone teasing you?" She sighed.

"I just want to know because I think I am starting to remember some of those things."

"Oh Stasia." She stared at me until she realized this really was important to me.

"Pa and I tucked you in for bed one night. We were already outside at the table when we heard you talking loudly. Pa ran into your room, which was downstairs at the time, and you were sitting up in bed, your eyes stiff and your mouth wide. Your hair was a mess and you'd looked like you just had a nightmare. You kept asking what had happened to the animals. Pa hugged you and tried to calm you, but you didn't like that. This wasn't the first nightmare you'd had about dragons. Your words were fast and your expressions kept changing. You were trying to tell us something but we could not understand. Your face was clammy. You threw our arms off like you didn't know us at all."

"So, what do you think happened?" I asked.

"We don't know. It all changed when we brought you to the museum one day to see the dragon skeleton. It was the first day you felt at ease. After that, you seemed to be content. Dr. Rose visited with you every day and you started to become acquainted with your surroundings. You started to speak more and more and eventually you were okay. You were back to normal." Mama gave me a sympathetic smile. "And see, you're almost normal now!" She tried to make light of the story, this time a big grin spread across her face. If she only knew what was *really* going on. All I could think about was telling Amelie that the events I had described when she first hypnotized me were the same ones Mama just told me. The hypnosis had worked and I had been recalling the night Pa had come into my room as a child after my nightmare. I hadn't been accepting my life in St. Michael, because I believed I should have still been living in Surritz. But what about the second time? Had I really regressed to my past life as Nina, to the day of my death?

Mama then hugged me and I did feel safe. I sank into her arms as if I were a little girl again.

"You've even gotten rid of your imaginary friends." She laughed. "I think!"

I smiled gently. "I had imaginary friends?" I'd always read about them in books but never thought that kids actually had them.

"Well, just one really," Mama replied, scratching my back. "Or maybe he is still around?" she said sarcastically, shaking her head and widening her eyes.

"Abe? Abe Carlton... You still here Abe?" she laughed.

CHAPTER 9

I TOSSED and turned for most of the night. Click. Click. Click. My alarm clock randomly tried to suck water into its pipes throughout the night but was unsuccessful. Nightmares littered my mind every time I dozed off. In one of them, Abe was a dragon with sharp, crooked teeth, chasing me down trying to eat me. In another, he was a blood-sucking vampire who was thirsty for my innocence. Internally, I wrestled with myself as I tried to refrain from running to the warm beach and going back to Surritz to ask Billy what was happening. Once dawn broke, I couldn't sit still anymore. I needed to find answers.

I SPOTTED Billy lounging behind a large coconut palm tree in Surritz. I could tell it was Billy by the red colored energy that he had vibrating above his tail. He noticed me immediately and set the orange he was playing with on the floor.

"Second time not so bad right?" he said, getting up to greet me.

"I met a lot of fish on the way down. Do they ever

get out of the spout?"

"The spout forms around anyone who is in the vicinity. Once the spout disappears, they are free to roam the ocean again," he said.

I nodded as if I understood. But, really, the concept was so foreign to me that it was hard to believe I had actually experienced it at all.

"They are the ones who are supposed to help you make the transition. But, sometimes they get lazy," he admitted.

I tried to figure Billy out but it was hard. He didn't change his expressions much. He always looked at me when I was talking but I felt like he was looking *through* me. He was listening, but I could tell he was also thinking about so many things at once. At times he seemed to be calculating different scenarios and then he was back in my presence smiling. Occasionally, his purple tongue whipped out of his mouth like a snake. I tried to compare him to the images and lectures about Wayters in my classes in Puncchit, but nothing about their looks or personalities were similar. Wayters are not supposed to be able to think. "Their instinctual drive is only to survive," I recalled the professor saying. So why was Billy here talking to me? And dare I say, in a sweet, sympathetic tone.

I figured he must know Abe, and that all this had to be connected. But when I told him what Mama said about my imaginary friend, he just opened his lips slightly before sighing. "So he found you long ago. But, as I said, no one can force you to remember. We all have free will, Stasia."

He picked up the orange and continued throwing it in the air like a baseball. His claws cusped gently around it as it went from hand to hand. I knew he wasn't going to reveal

Abe's identity anytime soon. So why did he bring me here? What was the point?

"You know," he said, juice dripping from his claws, "if you want to remember, you can ask the Tree of Waking Thoughts." He pointed to a large weeping willow in the distance. "It holds all your memories as it was the tree of your life in Surritz."

"What does it do?" I asked him.

"Each branch corresponds to a different time in your life. When you touch a leaf, you will fall into a deep sleep, and you'll be transported to that moment in your past life, looking at the world as the person you once were."

"Like I am experiencing it again?" I asked Billy.

"Yes. Your mind will travel back in time. But, your body will be fast asleep."

He caught my fearful expression. "Nothing can harm you. The Tree of Waking Thoughts is a very safe place. It's *your* tree. No one can bother you there. Just enjoy it, but remember, you can't change the past. You can only experience it as it happened."

And with that last word, Billy fluttered away again and went picking pears off a neighboring tree. I stared at the weeping willow for a while before moving. I remembered it from my dreams. It was the one I was walking towards. Even from afar, it was so big it made all of the nearby cottages look miniature.

There was a path to "my" tree so I followed along the beaten down trail that lead to it. The grassy plain turned into a rainforest and I found myself following the path deep into the woods. Different than any other path I had ever seen, it was not made of car tracks or animal footprints; it was a path of dirt triangles.

As I continued navigating through the wooded area, the rainforest changed to a field of sunshine and flowers and then to low hanging fog with mossy green trees. I could no longer see my tree in the distance but I felt sure that I was going towards it. Different colored pebbles lay on the ground below my feet and in the bushes nearby. I had expected them to be the energy gems, but when I picked one up, it started to move. They were, instead, some sort of beetle. They crawled up my arms and flew out of my hands leaving a colored trail in the air behind them. Picking up more and more bugs, I stuffed them into my palms and released them all at once to create a colored shooting star effect.

As I continued, the air got so thick I could barely see through it. I shivered as the temperature lowered to a chilly breeze. My clothes were heavy and wet and I fought to raise each leg and continue walking.

Finally, I saw green light in the distance and the tree came into view again. It was bigger than five of St. Michael's palm trees combined. From the branches hung little white leaves that glimmered like light bulbs. Reaching out to touch one, I immediately felt a sort of familiarity with the tree. I crawled under the branches pushing leaves out of my way until I saw the old trunk. To my surprise, a little seat had been carved into it. It was not just an indentation, but rather an actual chair with a line pattern on the back and seat. The tree was so large that I could not see anything once I was under it. The "tree cave" was the most peaceful place I had been in a long time.

As I sat in the wooden tree chair, I could feel the energy of memories surround me. I touched the closest golden leaf and the name Nina rang in my mind.

Images of a very beautiful girl with long brown hair

and strikingly blue eyes hovered in front of me. Her hair was blowing and her lips kept moving. Her eyes blinked, her head nodded, and I thought of Amelie who looked similar. Was I at one point actually as beautiful as she? I was relieved and surprised to see no disgusting birthmark on Nina's neck. I enjoyed looking at the images of this girl. I *felt* the emotions that I carried with me in that lifetime. They were dominated by peace and love, but there was some worry and regret. Uneasiness.

I switched my thoughts to Abe Carlton and suddenly a branch blew my way and a bright, glowing leaf hung in front of my face. I reached out to grab it and touched it lightly with my fingertips. Images of a man floated into my mind.

He had dark tanned skin, a chiseled jaw, and mes-merizing brown eyes. I blinked several times, hoping to catch a better view. He remained still and unmoving before many images started to appear in my head. One after another, they flooded my mind until they seemed to be connecting, moving. As I watched the movies play out in my mind, I became very tired, until suddenly, I was transported back in time. I was Nina.

CHAPTER 10

I SIT by the mossy covered lake pushing in the parts of water that have frozen. Particles break and float away from my fingertips. It was only a couple years ago that Surritz was introduced to ice. I was twelve years old at the time, and I spent hours at Blootea volcano playing with the frozen sheets of water.

Blootea volcano is usually spitting fire, but rarely do we see it shoot out ice. However, when this rare occasion occurs, everyone leaves home to collect it from the lake before it melts. Very few times in history has this happened, but I attribute it to the fact that today is the day. Today is the day that Abe is to return from Earth.

I play with the ice, running it slowly over my lips, tasting the cooling sensation over my tongue. When I bite into it, my teeth ache so I take it out and skip it over parts of the lake that haven't iced over yet, careful not to knock over the swans.

The weather slowly starts changing. The ocean stirs up the sand and it is no longer clear. When I look around, I am incapable of seeing anything but a milky brownish-gray color in the waters surrounding Surritz. The mixed up ocean water almost blocks the sunlight completely. Even though it is daytime, it is very dark at 10 AM. A chilly breeze howls by my shoulder. When I lie down under the blanket I brought with me this morning, I hear the sound. Ding, Ding, Dong. The bell in the city only rings for special occasions. I know what this one is for. We all know. We have waited for this moment for two years.

I grab my backpack and stuff the blanket back inside with the water bottle and crackers I brought. I thought I'd be here for half the day, but it has only been one hour and I am already leaving. I care so much about Abe's return; I also know that if I am not there, everyone will be angry. I know this because I was the one who was with Abe the day he left. What would it look like if I am not there when he returns?

I start to run at top speed back through the forest that scares me; once, I got lost as a child when I wandered out of the house and the creatures I saw in the forest still haunt me. But it was the only way to get to the hidden lake. I discovered it when I was forced to find my dog Bisket who ran away. I looked for hours on end, screaming her name like a lost child looking for her mother.

I breathe in and out slowly. My slim body has no trouble and I actually enjoy the jog. It is a bit harder than usual because of the fog and cold weather, but I can manage.

I knew I wouldn't be able to stand having to be around all the people in the town square, waiting endlessly for Abe to return. So I faced my fear of the forest head on to get to the lake that no one knew about. Only an hour later, I face the forest again.

What is the big deal with Abe returning? What do they think he is bringing back anyway?

I think about him and about the way we met shortly before he discovered the funnel in the ocean. I was with him that day. He said he thought he saw something unusual with the needlefish hovering in one spot in the water. It was a sunny day and the sea was still. As far as we could see in each direction, even the fish were not moving. However, ten needlefish gathered around a certain spot and one by one they disappeared; they got sucked up into 'something' so fast, that before we knew it, they were all gone.

Abe went to investigate, of course. He was a tough guy with no fears. For someone as young as he was, even younger than me by three days, he should've been scared of something. He called himself an old soul, whatever that meant. But I believed him.

I stop by my house on the way to the town square. It is dark and all I can see are the lights that shine through the windows, but I know no one is home. Aunt Agnes and Uncle Pete left at the same time as I did this morning just so they wouldn't miss the 'return'. Everyone is so curious to know what Abe has experienced. For a whole year, we thought he drowned. He was a good swimmer, but as far as we knew, there was nothing else out there beyond miles and miles of ocean. His parents mourned. Abe and I had just met prior to his "departure", but I mourned too. I didn't understood the feelings, but now I think that it was just because I felt guilty for letting him go into the ocean.

I enter my house briefly to change clothes. Aunt Agnes and Uncle Pete warned that I should dress up for the occasion.

"He could be bringing you a gift," my aunt said, patting down my frizzy hair.

I grab the headband I left on my bureau this morning.

The soft white feather brushes against my face before I secure it in my hair. I made the headband last week and it is the first time that I am getting to wear it. I am actually proud of how good it looks.

Before I can apply some lip wax, I hear the sound again. Ding, Ding, Dong. The second warning. It is louder and faster—a sign that everyone should hurry into the city as soon as possible.

I am out the door in less than five minutes. The city is only another ten minutes' walk so I have plenty of time to meet up with my aunt and uncle. I decide to skip the streets and take a shortcut I found—a dusty trail through the fields. Some know about it, but it remains mostly undiscovered.

As I go into a slow jog again, I think about what Abe said to me before he entered the ocean.

If I don't come back, take care of Toro.

Then he laughed. We both did. But did he have a premonition? I often thought that he was a clairvoyant. There was something strange about Abe. Even from the first day we met, he knew things. He knew about things. Somehow he knew the secret lake. He knew when I'd be there. He even knew my name, who my family was, and where I lived.

But even though we joked about him not coming back, I honored his last comment as if it really was his last wish.

I didn't have the heart to tell Abe's parents what he said, so I just asked politely if I could have Toro. I used the excuse that I'd grown fond of him since Abe brought him along wherever he went. They were fine with the idea. They didn't know how to take care of a water dragon anyway.

When I approach the city, the bright lights make it easier for me to see my way around. Crowds of people stand in groups drinking wine and catching up with old friends. I know the location where Aunt Agnes and Uncle Pete are sitting, so I head over to the town square. Colored towels are spread out all over the lawns. People applaud as they see me. They call me by my full name, Potnia, which makes me cringe. I have never liked the name.

"It's Nina," I say to one of them before more and more people gather around me.

"Cheers to Potnia!" screams a drunk lady.

"Pot-ni-a. Pot-ni-a. Pot-ni-a," they all chant.

I guess I turned into a sort of celebrity because I was the one who fished out the note from the ocean. The note from Abe.

This wasn't the only thing that came out of the ocean. Before Abe left, he found a Polaroid camera on the sand. We didn't know what it was at first, but once we started snapping, we figured out quickly that it captured our images on the paper. The ocean continued to spit out objects: candles, silverware, soggy books, gold, clothing, and even small furniture!

"What did it say!" a man declares.

"Yes, read it to us again."

"Potnia. Potnia!" They continue faster.

When I fished the note out of the water one day by the secret lake, I could have sworn a needlefish handed it to me. I figured that the needlefish that got sucked up went to the same place that Abe did, but maybe one figured out how to return. But with a note? This was obviously impossible. The little note traveled in a bottle all the way from Abe directly to where I was standing that day. It seemed like an almost impossible coincidence. Fish were not smart enough to "bring things." They didn't even have any way of carrying it.

I didn't intentionally memorize the note, but after the fifth time of having to recite it, it is ingrained in my mind.

"POOOOTNIA," a baby cries, mimicking her father.

"Okay, are you ready?" I ask, getting all of them riled up. They quiet down so they can hear me. I begin to recite the letter.

"I'm sorry for making you worry. I am very much alive. I know it has been a year but I did not know how to send word back to Surritz. I have reached Earth! I just celebrated my nineteenth birthday. I have only now learned how to return. I will be back on June 9th. Look for me, wait for me.
That's all for now.
Abe"

"Potnia, Potnia!" The crowd keeps chanting.

I finally spy my aunt and uncle at the back of the crowd. I smile as I fight through the people to reach them. There's only one thing I leave out from the letter. It is the only thing that told me that the letter was directed to me specifically. And it is the one thing I feel guilty about.

Toro disappeared a week after Abe left. I wasn't crazy about dragons in the first place. I looked for him but I could have looked harder. I had a lot more love for Bisket that I had willingly ventured into my fear of the forest to find her. But Toro? I didn't go into the woods for him.

So what is Abe going to ask me today when I see him, when the last question on his letter was, *How is Toro?*

CHAPTER 11

THE WAITING seems endless. Uncle Pete starts to fidget. Even my aunt, who is polite and proper, starts to move restlessly on her towel. The town is ringing the bells as if Abe is returning at any moment. But in fact, they have no way of knowing when he will return; his letter said nothing about a time. I guess they just want everyone in the square when it happens.

The ocean water is churning, letting less sunlight through. Some streaks of color light up faintly, but only from the glow fish who are being tossed around in the waves.

The color in the air is that of dusk, but it is rapidly declining into nightfall. It is now 3 PM. If I thought people were drunk before, now they are truly intoxicated. However, there is less noise because they are getting tired. Most are not on their feet anymore. The colored blankets are now covered with bodies, some sleeping. I look to my aunt and uncle again; they are still sitting upright on theirs.

We spent the first two hours constantly looking around in the ocean in all directions, hoping not to miss anything. Now, we sit with our backs to each other. Aunt

Agnes looks in the direction of east, my uncle looks to the west, and I lean my head against his shoulder staring around at the top of the ocean. The town officials have also gotten tired and have retreated to their stations in the municipal building.

I stretch out my legs, staring at my brown leather shoes. I only wear them on special occasions. Did I put them on for Abe? I have mixed feelings about him. Maybe it is because we met under strange circumstances.

I remember the day like it was yesterday. After fighting with my uncle about being late for school, I took off and ran straight into my worst nightmare—the forest. I was so upset with him that I didn't care if the creatures ripped me to threads. I wanted to get away from him, away from all his lecturing. Instead of taking the quick route that I always took to the secret lake, I ran the other direction. In case he knew where I had always been going, I didn't want to stand a chance that he would come and find me.

The other direction led straight to a small abandoned castle. Ivy grew along the sides of the stone walls, making it look almost like a large bush. Only the wooden door was visible. At first, I thought I was seeing things. The architecture of the building was different than anything else I had seen in Surritz. It must have been centuries old.

My curiosity got the best of me. I forgot about the dangerous forest and I stepped up to the front door, running my fingers over the outside of it. Despite the hot, sticky humidity in the air, the door was cold and dry. Small animals were carved into the wood. I felt each indentation, closing my eyes to guess what animal I was feeling.

Before I was done, the door opened slightly and a smell similar to the citrus potpourri Aunt Agnes placed in our living room hit me. The scent reminded me so much of home that I had no problem opening the door completely and stepping inside. It was dark and the place seemed empty.

"Where am I?" I asked.

An answer came back at me. "Hello? Hello? Who's there?"

Dim lights flickered on in an instant. Surprisingly, I wasn't afraid. Maybe it was because of what I saw next. Animals.

They were walking around the castle slowly, in groups of two or more. I figured there was a back entrance. Perhaps the castle was broken down and opened to a place where the animals ventured in. But surely, I had heard a man call to me.

"Hello?" I asked. "Where are you?"

I walked past some of the animals, which looked at me but didn't move. Their eyes met mine directly. Horses, zebras, goats, cows, and a human. A man!

He was sitting on the floor, petting a squirrel that was staring at a set of cards in front of him.

"I'm sorry." I stumbled backwards. "I just let myself in. I didn't know it was…occupied."

He looked embarrassed and got to his feet quickly.

My first thought was, *is he homeless?*

But he was young. I noticed how clean he looked and how his clothes fit him perfectly. A pair of navy blue pants contrasted with his white t-shirt.

"No, it's okay," he answered.

"What are you doing?" I asked as if I already knew him.

"Well, I just come here to relax and think," he answered before I asked him about the animals.

"They invaded this place. I followed one in the woods

one day and he led me here. I never knew this place existed. When I entered, I found all these animals hanging out!" He laughed revealing a strong, structured jaw and a perfectly imperfect set of white teeth. "I'm Abe, by the way."

I didn't press him for more answers, although I had a lot more questions…

"Nina, Nina!" Aunt Agnes shakes me. "Look!"

A body! It is floating through the ocean on the east side. I should have known that Abe would be coming back on that side; it was the same side he left on!

I look around and notice that almost no one else sees what we do. They are too busy snoring.

"Let's go over there," my uncle whispers, as if it's our secret.

"Shouldn't we tell the officials?" my aunt asks, wanting to obey the rules that were set before anyone was allowed to enter the town square.

"Oh, if they were so concerned, they would have been out here with us all day," my uncle replies.

We are up on our feet, along with a few others who notice the same object in the water. A group of about fifteen of us are walking towards the dark shadow in the water that seems to be getting closer and closer to land.

My heart starts to beat faster and adrenaline begins to shoot through my body. I hope that Abe is okay and that he was not hurt or tortured on his journey. Different scenarios run through my mind as I envision someone forcing him to write the letter only because they want to invade Surritz. I had never seen Abe's handwriting before; perhaps it really wasn't him at all who wrote the letter. Maybe it isn't even him we are all staring at in the water right now!

As we approach the ocean side, the area outside gets brighter and brighter. Glow fish gather around the body and are swimming crazily in all directions. It is still rather quiet, but when I look back, I see that our footsteps are waking others as well. They don't seem to see what we are seeing. Most lie back down, turning around on their towels to face the other way. Surely if they saw the body, they would have gotten up and started to run over.

There is a loud splash in the ocean and something comes tumbling out. My uncle grabs my hand to pull me away from the water but something large already fell at my feet. The ocean starts to pour out on top of it like a faucet. All of us part and step back. A few brave men go towards the ocean, thinking that somehow their hands can stop the flow of water, but it keeps spewing out. Did Abe punctured a hole in gravity? The men stumble around, splashing the ocean water, hoping to get the cycle to return to normal. No one dares to help the man who is now underneath the spout for fear that he may drown.

As we collectively fight to stop the flood of seawater, it starts to sting my eyes. I have to step back because I can't see anything.

Then, I hear someone scream, "Wayter!"

When I open my eyes, the ocean has screened off the hole and on the ground lies a baby water dragon flapping around; it is panicking and screaming. He hasn't lived on land yet, because he is too young to breathe air for long periods of time. His purple tongue whips around in the air like a loose electrical wire.

The brave men once again move in quickly.

"Everyone, take a position around him," one shouts.

"We can hoist him back in."

"Let's do it now."

Uncle Pete springs into action and goes to the dragon's rear, carefully trying to get a grip without being struck by its tail. But the water dragon is slippery and no one can get a hold of it as it moves frantically.

Its screams travel through my body.

Please little one, please, you have to get back into the ocean, I pray. *It's okay, it's okay! Just stop moving. I know what you are. Toro is a Wayter too.*

I am squeezing my eyes shut so tightly that I begin to see stars.

The commotion starts to die down quickly. I open my eyes but only see a white-gray color as I try to regain my vision.

"He's calm," one of the men says.

Oh no, he's dying, I think but do not say aloud.

"Is he breathing?" my aunt asks.

"Yes, he's breathing. He seems okay," my uncle responds.

The dragon's dark eyes peer at me, rolling from left to right.

They all agree to try to lift him again. This time the two men, who have since sobered up quickly, grab each fin while my uncle holds the tail. The baby must be at least one hundred pounds, but between the three men, they move quickly towards the ocean wall.

"On three," says the taller man.

"One," they count in unison.

"Two."

By three, they lift the baby dragon into the ocean and encourage him to swim. He rushes into the water and is gone in an instant.

"Thank goodness he suddenly calmed down," Aunt Agnes says, relieved. "He would have died had he kept thrashing around."

I want to take credit considering that I was probably the only one who prayed. But something else wanders into my mind. Something silly, but I keep thinking about it...
Could he have read my mind?

CHAPTER 12

EVERYONE IS still sitting on the ground breathing rapidly. We are all so preoccupied with why the dragon fell out of the ocean that not one of us thinks that it may have had something to do with Abe. In fact, I forgot about Abe altogether! Until, I notice it.

A hand. A hand!

"A hand!" I scream.

It's a shock to all of us. A hand is reaching out of the water. The water is churned up and we can't see anything else. It's like a hand coming out of a wall.

It moves slowly and we all cautiously go towards it.

"Abe?" whispers the tall man to the other.

"I don't know. Let's be careful," he answers.

The arm is sticking out of the water and we discuss pulling at it but then decide that it is not the best idea to do so.

I am hoping I can recognize the hand and nails. After all, I am closer to Abe than any of the people around me. I move closer to the still hand and arm that is sticking out of the ocean. I examine it from all angles, but I don't recognize anything. I am still pretending that I might when suddenly the hand starts twitching.

"Move away!" my uncle scolds. "Nina, what are you doing?"

Then, a right leg comes out and starts waving in the air until it touched the ground firmly.

"Just pull it out!" the short man says.

So the two men, along with my uncle, yank the lively body out of the water. It is Abe!

"Abe!" I scream. I cannot control myself as I run to hug him. I don't know what causes that reaction, but suddenly I am so happy to see him.

He looks just as he did the day he left. Maybe I thought Earth would distort his features or warp his body, but he is the same. He is the same boy who left two years ago.

"You like that, the moving hand?" he says. "Wish I could have taken a picture of your faces! It was priceless."

The two older men are embarrassed, but my aunt and uncle seem relieved.

"You saw us?" I ask.

"Yes, clear as day. Like a piece of clean glass."

"And the Wayter?" the tall man asks.

"That was an accident. He was bringing me back from Earth so quickly and the water was so clear, he miscalculated the distance a little. I was thrown off as he tried to slide to a halting stop."

We all have so many questions for Abe but no one is saying anything; we are all in shock.

"That's it? Only a few came for my return? I thought the letter would have had a greater effect on Surritz," Abe says.

But then his eyes shift to the back of us. I turn around and notice that all the drunken zombies have come back to life. Their noise gets louder and louder as crowds of people run and clap, scream and jump. Finally they realize they missed the event that they came for.

It is dusk by the time everyone calms down. Abe is very patient. He goes from family to family, shaking hands with children and spending time talking to parents. *He really is a celebrity*, I think. As I watch him confidently throw his hands into the air, telling a tale to two little children, I suddenly become aware that something inside me was absent from the time he left. The feeling fills by body again and I finally realize that I have been missing him much more than I thought. There is a sense of security in my bones again. He is only twenty, but he is very tall for his age. Actually, he is taller than the average man, and I feel like a little girl standing next to him.

I wait my turn, anxious to speak to him, but there are too many people around. I know he will never talk freely right now, which is okay, because I still haven't come up with an excuse about Toro.

When he finally finishes with most of the people in the crowd, he backs up to the ocean and signals everyone to sit down. Silence reigns over us. Glow fish light up the ocean on all sides as they fight to get a peek at what is going on. Before Abe is able to say anything, someone screams out from the crowd, "Tell us how you did it Abe. We all know about your letter. How'd you leave Surritz? How did you find Earth?"

Before the clapping and hollering starts, I want to get up and answer the question for him. I want to tell them how simple it was, that I was there that day and that I know. But no one knows I was there. My aunt and uncle thought it better to keep it a secret so I wouldn't have people asking me questions, surrounding me daily, and blaming me if he didn't return.

"Someone told me about the secret passage and when I decided to pursue it, it actually happened to be true," says Abe.

What? I am puzzled for a moment. Why is he lying? I was there and it was as simple as a step on the wrong rock. I look him straight in the eye without moving, hoping to search his face for answers. But there are none in his expression. He does not even glance my way.

"Tell us what happened? How did you come back? Did you want to?" The same man screams, still clearly intoxicated. His wife tries to calm him down with a quick, "Hush!"

Lots of animals begin to mix with the crowd. A few mongooses run behind Abe and stand on their hind legs, curiously watching him. I spot a couple goats that have invaded the empty beach towels. Foxes peek out from the bushes. Birds flutter around the trees, chirping loudly.

I think back again to the day I met Abe. He had given the animals in the castle names and introduced me to all of them.

"What's better than a man who loves animals?" he asked.

Was that an invitation? To love him? I remember my stupid response. "One who loves people? Girls?"

"Don't worry, I love girls too," he said.

He showed me around the small castle as the animals followed. The front of it was right in the middle of the woods, but all of its other sides were surrounded by beautiful gardens full of herbs, vegetables, and wild flowers. He took me through a path he carved, while picking ripe berries and tossing them in his mouth.

Once we were in this garden, I did not feel like I was in the woods anymore. The woods were full of danger. Every moment in the forest kept me on my toes, full of anxiety. The dark branches of trees lurked around every corner, housing unexpected death traps—poisonous foods, animals ready to attack, and mud that tried to cement its victims. The vast open area felt like a region I could not escape.

But this, this peaceful small garden presented the opposite feeling. It was bright and inviting. I was able to see over the tallest bush, but when I sat down in the field I was surrounded by the scents of new leaves and tropical trees. Someone had kept the place nicely organized. The grass was cut in certain areas and fresh dirt had been placed around newly sprouting vegetables.

"You never told me how you found this place," Abe interrupted my thoughts.

Did I want to tell him how I just stumbled upon it while running through the forest in no direction? No.

"You never asked," I replied coyly.

"I just mean, it's so far back in the woods most people don't bother to venture out here."

"Where are we going anyway?" I asked.

The animals were still following behind us, very eager to get to where Abe was taking us. They didn't seem to mind that I was tagging along...

"Where did I go?" Abe asks the crowd that is now very restless. "I ended up in a place that is very similar to our own...except this place, on Earth, is above all water."

People look at Abe like they don't understand what he is saying.

"It's not possible," one screams out.

"Don't fool us!" says a child.

Abe only chuckles, somehow putting the crowd at ease.

I thought he would surely change because he was in a different world, but he is still the same boy I met at the castle. He has the same beautiful smile and confidence to accompany it. But not once has he looked at me. Is he ignoring me? Does he know about Toro?

"It was absolutely amazing. The air came from the heavens. You can look for miles and miles into the atmosphere. And the land is *above* the water, not around it like Surritz," he says.

I try to imagine what that must be like, but my mind is blank. I look around to see the same expression on everyone else's faces. Shock.

Then Abe explains how he got there. It was only seconds of travel before he appeared in the middle of a lake. He was able to swim to shore, bobbing his head above the water like the glow fish that stick their tails out of the ocean side when they are excited.

"Of course, I didn't come back empty handed," says Abe.

My aunt and uncle stand by my side, each holding one of my hands. Aunt Agnes gives me a little smirk and a nod; she thinks that Abe brought something back for me.

Abe reaches into his pocket and pulls out a little sealed box. The animals surrounding him already sense that something is wrong. Some make noises while others scamper away or back up against the bushes. It reminds me of the instincts they possess, always being able to sense danger before it's near. We rely on the animals to let us know when the sea is getting angry and rough so that we can board up our houses before a flood.

When Abe opens the box, he tilts it to show the crowd. Surrounded by soft red velvet lining, a small shiny rock gleams back at us.

"The white diamond," Abe says slowly, trying to speak as if the stone is not dangerous, but his worried expression tells otherwise.

Its crystal clear sparkle allows no one to take his or her eyes off of it.

Only a select few in the front row get to touch and smell the rock. As each one does, he steps back with an expression of surprise on his face. A feeling of delight. A surge of happiness.

"Because the intentions of the people on Earth have become greedy, their negative thoughts have manifested into this rock on their universe. Their sinful thinking has actually transitioned into this tangible object. The more greed and less love these people have, the more this object will destroy their planet. It is against everything made by nature—it can freeze and kill all forms of life," Abe says.

"What are you saying?" a young girl asks.

"I guarantee their universe will shrivel up from sheer cold and life will die," says Abe.

"Is that why you came back?" asks another.

"It's already starting. Species of animals are becoming extinct. Plants are dying. The weather is turning. Their thoughts have manifested into real life forms of negative energy."

Finally, when I am starting to get angry at his ignoring

me, Abe peers down at me in the front row.

"Maybe you can feel the vibrations in this stone, Nina."

I reach out wanting to touch his hand more than anything, but I contain the urge to grab him and pull him closer to me.

"It doesn't hold powers, Abe. It's just energy. Like everything else," I reply before I touch it, as if I know better than he does.

"No, no, no. It's not like the yellow diamond in Surritz. The white diamond reflects colors. It doesn't possess any," he says.

Again, people gasp. I see the fear that rushes from face to face. People turn to each other, trying to console one another, trying to pretend that what Abe has said is not true. It can't be.

I slowly extend my hand to touch the stone. It's small and cold in my palm. Almost immediately, waves of energy surge up my arm and I feel the shock of electricity in my bones. Different emotions run through my body. I feel beautiful, confident, careful, powerful, competitive, and avaricious.

CHAPTER 13

I HAVE never felt those emotions before, at least not altogether. I still have not gotten a chance to talk to Abe alone. When he got tired of addressing everyone, he left with his family to rest, and I went back to wandering around Surritz, not satisfied with my decisions about the diamond.

Now, at nightfall, I go to the only place I keep thinking about—the old castle where I met Abe. I don't bother to enter through the front door. I take the path around to the back gardens, the place where all the animals followed Abe to get to the barn where he fed them.

The glow fish are on full swing. They have all the light they can possess and they dot the ocean like thousands of small lights twinkling. There is a peaceful energy in the air now that Abe has returned and I feel myself unwinding a little as I pass the herb garden. Shadows of eggplants and tomatoes reflect on the ground. Even at night, the garden is a place of security.

When I finally see the barn, it is lit up with one lamp that is bent over the tip of the door. This is where Abe tried to coax me into believing it was where he lived…

"Finally, here," he said, still chewing raspberries. I started to feel uneasy. No one knew I was there.

"I should get back," I said.

"Don't be scared, you'll love this."

I reluctantly followed him inside while all the animals bombarded us, squeezing themselves through the door, oinking, mooing, and growling with delight.

The inside of the barn was set up like a circus. Different colored drapes hung from the ceiling. Hay was on the floor. Fresh apples dangled from the walls.

As each animal took his place in the room, Abe walked around feeding them, talking to them slowly. I watched his hands gently caress the backs of the animals and they turned around slowly to lick his face or nudge his body.

"You feed them?" I asked. "All of them?"

He turned around to give me a side smile. "They count on me."

It was almost an hour by the time he was done with the feeding. The animals were so comfortable with his presence. They rolled around on their backs, playing with each other...

As I stand in the barn now, it is gently lit with a few dim candles but no animals are in sight. There is a smell that I recognize from the last time. It smells like burnt rubber mixed with a little bit of garlic. *Skunks*, I remember. That is what they smell like.

As I make my way around the stone walls to the back, I notice that the barn is larger than I think. Long hallways jut off in different directions. Each one is candlelit and lined with fresh carnations.

I hope to see Abe here, even though I figure that he is sound asleep in his house by now. Questions I want answered fill my mind.

Why did he lie about the way he found the funnel?
Why was he short about the place he's been to on Earth?
Was he not happy to see me?
Had he missed me at all?

As the questions roll around in my mind, I suddenly notice that I finished walking down the long hall and am now in a smaller room. A fireplace stands in the far corner and small burning flames drift away from it. I could hear the wind in the barn, but in this room, there is only silence with the occasional cracking of wood. Someone must be here. But where? I hadn't encountered even one animal since my arrival.

"Nina," a voice calls out after a few minutes. His voice. I had heard it in my mind for months even though he's been gone.

"Abe?" I turn around to face the direction in which I hear his words. Then I see him. "What are you doing here?" I ask, only half surprised.

"I should ask you that," he says as his face comes into view. I wait to see if he smiles. He does, and I am so relieved.

"I'm so glad to see you," I manage to say.

I want to run to him. After all the time he's been away, I still haven't gotten a hug. I barely even got a word. Aren't we closer than that? I thought so, but now I wonder. It's been a long time. Long enough for him to change his mind about me.

"I just needed to get away from all the people," he says.

"Away from me?"

"You're the only one I was looking forward to seeing. You're the reason I came back."

I didn't know I was holding my breath until now when I release it. Abe sits on a couch opposite the fireplace. I wait for him to invite me to sit with him but he doesn't.

The fire keeps cracking. It is larger now, illuminating almost the entire room, which looks more or less like a living room.

"And because of what I saw," he adds.

"What?" I ask before I can't stand the suspense anymore. "Didn't you want to come back to see me? Why did you leave for so long? Didn't you think I would be worried?"

"Of course I did. You think I wanted to be there? To stay there? I didn't know how to get back. I didn't even know where I was."

Light from dusk permeates the room through the only small window above Abe's head. The dust in the air reflects off the rays as they slowly move towards the fire.

"What did you see?" I ask.

He pauses for a short moment, thinking to himself.

"When you look up, you see blue sky for miles. You can float on top of the water and breathe the air. It's just, a miracle."

He continued happily talking about the land for a long time. He explained how the trees were different, far less green, and taller than any trees we have in Surritz. He spoke of how the people had magical devices called phones for talking to each other, and telepathic TV boxes where they could transport to see each other. They drive around in electric powered vehicles that they created. They built the tallest brick buildings and had captured music that came out of the same boxes they used to teleport.

It sounded unreal.

"What do the people look like?" I interrupt him.

"Basically the same," he says. "They wear similar clothes, only, much more of them. They talk like we do. If they get cut, they bleed. They are essentially the same person as you and I."

"No aliens?" I laugh.

Tales of aliens reached Surritz years ago. If there was any life outside of us, it was thought to be them. They were little green men with pointy ears and webbed hands. I didn't know where the myth had come from, but we all believed it.

"So you came back because you saw that? It sounds amazing," I say to Abe.

"They are nice like we are," he says, "but the difference is, they have an agenda."

"A daily schedule?"

He explains the word agenda. It means people who plot, steal, and even kill. All it takes a single thought.

"Do they really kill each other with their thoughts?" I ask.

"All they think about is killing," he replies.

For the rest of the afternoon into dark night, I learn more about the people on Earth. They think about themselves constantly. They are so obsessed with gaining more and more items that they spend every waking moment trying to figure out ways to spend their time working to get more and more money. They smile and laugh and tell stories like we do, but they are usually unhappy. They pretend to love, help, and be kind, but really, they hate. They operate out of a foreign attitude that has somehow permeated the whole race. They are, essentially, what we have also heard myths about. They are possessed. They are monsters. If they are angered enough, they will physically harm each other.

"It's only a matter of time until their land is gone," Abe explains. "So that's what I saw. That's why I had to find a way to come back."

When I press Abe for more details about how he knows they are destroying the land, he just says that the weather will keep getting colder and colder until they cannot survive.

When we both start to get really tired, I tell Abe that we should probably be getting home. He agrees, but not before saying, "Can I have a hug now?"

I quickly sink into his arms the same way I used to. The questions I want to ask him still roll around in my mind. I will ask him tomorrow. I can't ruin this moment, the one I feared I might never have again.

His fingers poke into my back strongly and he lays his head on mine. His soft curls brush against my warm cheek.

"I'm sorry I was acting so strange. I just needed to tell someone about what I saw in St. Michael," he says.

"St. Michael?" I ask.

"That was the name," he says to me before whispering to himself, "the inverted island."

I try to picture it in my head, but it seems so impossible that no real pictures come to mind.

CHAPTER 14

IN MY dreams that night, the images Abe described to me earlier roll around in my mind. I stand on an island staring up into the universe with nothing to protect me. There's no water above me, and no water to the side of me. It only surrounds the land, but it is so far below. I feel like I am on a cliff looking down at it roaring back up. I start running, trying to find Abe, but a metal box on wheels comes at lightning speed to block my path. Inside, people who look like humans are telling me to come with them. One girl jumps out of the car and showers me with jewelry. She pushes all of it in my hand, yelling at me to put it on. I even see the diamond Abe brought back in her palm. The others throw fancy clothes at me. They tell me that the box on wheels is mine to keep; it is far too old for them to keep using.

"Where's Abe? Where's Abe?" I scream but they ignore me. Their piercing, soulless eyes tell me that they are monsters. They start stroking my long dark hair and feel my thin body.

"I wish I had your body, Nina," says a fat lady in an orange dress.

"Yes, and this beautiful hair," adds the other one, who is equally as fat.

Their expressions all change. Suddenly, they throw all their possessions on the floor as they become more and more obsessed with me.

I'm in danger of being killed by their thoughts, I think.

But then it's all over because I wake up in my small bed in Surritz. The humidity has dampened my skin, and the tiny ceiling fan provides the same familiar clicking sound that it does every night.

Even though it was only a few hours earlier that Abe walked me home and personally tucked me into bed, I am insecure again and the questions come back to my mind.

Why did he lie about the way he found the funnel?
Why was he short about the place he's been to on Earth?
Was he not happy to see me?
Had he missed me at all?

He answered some of the questions, I remind myself. Maybe he just didn't feel comfortable telling all of Surritz about the monsters. He probably didn't want any more attention. He had been asked dozens of questions. He was probably just tired.

I turn over onto the other side of my pillow and I remember the inevitable question that he has still not asked: Where is Toro?

In the morning, I don't remember having any other dreams, but I do remember tossing and turning for the remainder of the night. It is the smell of bacon that lures me downstairs where I find my aunt and uncle chatting at the kitchen table.

"Good morning," Aunt Agnes says, "quite a day yesterday. I'm glad you got some rest."

She is wearing a blue and white plaid apron, and is fiercely flipping the bacon from side to side as smoke fills the small kitchen.

"Thanks," I say as my uncle follows the flipped bacon up and down as he waits for his turn to speak.

"So, did Abe tell you anything else?" he asks. "He was a bit short in town, having been gone two years."

"He was tired of everyone poking and prodding him. I'm sure you would have been the same way," I reply defensively.

He agrees and asks again if I had heard anything else from Abe. His non-stop questions irritate me, but I figure they do have a right to be interested. Everyone was interested. Why would they not be?

I decide not to tell them anything. If Abe wanted to tell anyone else, he would have. As we sit down to eat breakfast, the sun beams through the window onto the crispy meat and fresh eggs. Aunt Agnes and Uncle Pete try to convince me to go fishing today so they can cook fish for supper.

"Would be a pleasant dinner, don't you think Nina?" says Aunt Agnes. "You know your uncle would be happy to take you fishing."

"We could go right after breakfast. The weather is beautiful and the ocean clear," Uncle Pete says.

I say I am not feeling well. I lie, because all I can think about is getting back to Abe and finding out what else he saw in St. Michael. Surely, if my aunt and uncle knew I was being trusted with information about Earth, they would gladly encourage me to see Abe.

When I meet up with him at noon as planned, it is by the secret lake in the forest. He is in a better mood today and

I can tell that he is well rested. He prepared a picnic of bread, cheese, and juice—all laid out on the blanket for when I arrived.

"Thought we could chat over fine wine and cheese," he says in an accent I don't recognize, perhaps one from St. Michael.

I encourage him with a smile and sit down next to him.

"Seriously though. There is something I want to talk to you about," he says.

A slight breeze brushes against my bare arms and looking up, I notice that many geese are gliding along the lake. I spot a few monkeys in the trees and some hippos in the water! Three cows are across the pond!

"Wow! There's a lot of anima—" I begin to say but he interrupts me by laughing uncontrollably.

I open my mouth to ask him what he wants to say, but before I can, I notice three Wayters swimming by in the water. *Toro!* I remember. He will ask now. I know it.

"Nina," Abe says as I hold my breath, "How is Toro? I haven't seen him. Did you look after him when I was gone?"

Hardly, I think before quickly shaking my head to distract the words from flowing out of my mouth.

"Yes... I mean, I tried. I really did," I say.

Confusion splashes on his face as he digests my words.

The day Toro ran away flashes in my mind. Part of me was so angry Abe left me alone that when I watched Toro run into the forest, I didn't follow. I should have. I feel the guilt show up on my face in red splotches.

"What happened? Where is he?" Abe asks as his voice

cracks.

"I did watch him. I tried. He ran away, Abe. He barely let me even touch him. Every time I did he spit fire into the air. He must have known you were gone. There was just no way to stop him."

There is a pause before Abe tells me that Toro was a very important part of his life. I barely let him explain before I say, "I do understand. When Bisket left, I was heartbroken."

"It's different Nina," he says. "You may think there is something I am hiding from you. There is."

Why did you lie about the way you found the funnel? I want to say, but I let him speak.

"Toro made me realize my purpose," he says without further explanation. "Have you ever loved an animal before?"

I tell him the whole story about Bisket. Parts I have never told anyone before...

When the ocean revolted one day due to unknown circumstances, we were all forced to stay indoors for three full days. Fortunately, it was only the part of the ocean on top of Surritz that decided to produce waves that crashed down in sheets. If it had come from the sides of the ocean, we all could have been swept away. Drowned.

I just happened to be looking outside when I saw a small puppy clinging to a maple tree. She looked weak and close to being swept away by a stream of water. I could have remained inside but an emotion ran through my body. This emotion was one I never felt before but I instantly ran outside to rescue the dog. I brought her inside, cleaned off the dirt and muck on her coat, and made a little blanket for her to sleep in. Every morning she woke me up by kissing me, and every night she cuddled against my chest before she could even think of closing her eyes. The ways she thanked me for rescuing her needed no words. As she got older, her fear of the outdoors diminished and she started to feel comfortable enough to play in the garden. One day she saw a squirrel and decided she wanted to play with it. But the squirrel was so scared it started to run into the forest. I didn't think that Bisket would follow, but she did. It took all of my courage to run into the forest after her.

"Bisket, Bisket!" I yelled, panicking.

She usually came when I called her, but this time she had vanished. I walked around slowly taking in every new sense in the forest. Every noise, even the branches cracking under my own feet, made me jump.

"Bisket!" I screamed. I could not stay in the forest any longer for fear of a heart attack.

And then I heard it. Squeals.

"Bisket?"

They got louder and louder until I saw her. She had limped to find me. I dropped to my knees, examining her. There was a bite mark on the side of her body. Blood was coming out of her belly.

"No!" I cried. I picked up her small body, refusing to accept that she was dying.

I ran back through the forest as fast as I could, getting lost a few times until I finally spotted my house.

"Bisket!" I sobbed to Aunt Agnes who was standing in the doorway.

"Oh Nina," she reached for her, "she's gone."

She's gone. She's gone. The phrase played out in my head for months afterwards...

I start to cry again and Abe holds my hand. I haven't seen

Toro since Abe left. He must be dead by now, attacked in the forest like Bisket. Wayters have such trouble protecting themselves on land from bears and tigers. Their meat is delicious and a smart animal can attack from behind, inhibiting the dragon from breathing fire to protect itself. I sob a little harder and confess to Abe that I have been a bad person. I wronged him. I couldn't handle the only task he asked of me.

"Abe," I say in his arms, "please forgive me."

He doesn't. There is only silence.

When I finally look up through my tears, animals of all sorts and sizes are surrounding us. They have created a circle around the blanket we are sitting on.

I say Abe's name slowly. My first instinct tells me that the animals are there for the food. But inside I know that they are fed plenty every day in the barn.

They don't look unhappy or tense. Two small cats roll around in the grass playing with each other. A horse is trotting back and forth in the meadow. Goats start grazing. In the trees, birds line up on branches. I look to Abe again for an explanation, but he is eyeing something a half mile away. He squints as he slowly gets up. When the creature gets closer, I hear Abe whisper to himself, "Toro!"

He is up and running through the grass until he reaches the small dragon. He grabs Toro in his arms like a father who has found his lost child.

All the other animals surround them.

And then, can it be? Yes, from a distance, I hear it. The impossible happens; I hear Toro speak.

CHAPTER 15

MY HEAD throbbed as I stared at Dr. Rose.

"The thunder is making me jump. I can't concentrate," I said as yesterday's images flashed through my mind...

Waking up and panicking under the Tree of Waking Thoughts.

Jumping into the funnel.

Getting back to St. Michael.

Running home from the beach.

"Stasia, what you are having are lucid dreams. You wake up in your dreams at night and play out a fantasy, and then you believe that it's real. This stuff about another land underneath the sea, how can you believe something like that is true?"

We both sat in Dr. Rose's musty office in the back of his house. This was clearly the only room that wasn't renovated. Stacks of old books were piled high in the corners and rusty file cabinets were on the brink of collapse. The office seemed to not have been in use for a while. Even his desk was covered with old, water-stained papers from a leak in the roof. I spotted a few framed pictures of his family on the back windowsill.

"You've had this since you were little. You always played make-believe. But this is a really far-fetched—imaginary friend, land under the sea, colors that drift from your fingers in the water. Magical dragons? Your family is getting really worried."

"My dreams about Surritz are real. Surritz *is* underneath the ocean. And Amelie saw the colors from my fingers in the water too. Just ask her."

His dark eyes peered at me with pity. If he thought that was weird, what would he think if I told him I actually went to Surritz and re-lived parts of my life as Nina?

I decided against it. He was about to pat my back so I moved away.

"Amelie says you've been wandering around the yard, looking for footprints. That's why I decided to talk to you today. What have you really been doing?"

He leaned forward and pulled at his dark jacket like a real professional would do. He didn't believe me. He wasn't even considering it.

"When Amelie started telling me all this, I became gravely concerned," he continued. "You really haven't had any of this since you were a child and now it seems to be acting up again. Being a teenager is hard. I know you are out of your routine lately, and the dragon classes in Puncchit must have exacerbated your anxiety level, but I'm hoping the weather will let up a little bit and you can get back to a regular schedule."

I knew there was no hope in trying to convince him otherwise. At this point, he was tilting his head backwards and looking through his bifocals at a stack of papers in a manila file. Any hopes of not being treated like a mentally ill patient were shattered.

"Amelie, can you please come in here," Dr. Rose turned to the door.

Amelie walked into the room wearing one of her usual strange ensembles. Seeing her made me fidget. I wanted to tell her about the funnel to Surritz, and Abe, and how he had been to St. Michael in my past life. And everything he'd said about us—about our intentions and thoughts. About the energy and the weather. The monsters…were we those people now?

"Stasia says Surritz is a real place. Have you been there?" Dr. Rose asked.

Amelie glanced at me quickly. "Of course not, Daddy. It just got really scary. I was practicing life regression therapies on Stasia and she kept talking about this magical land. She keeps talking about a dragon named Billy that visits her in St. Michael. She's had too many of those stupid dragon classes in Puncchit."

I ran my fingers over my eyes, listening to the thunder crash in the sky. It was close—only 2 'one-thousand's' away.

I attempted to tell Dr. Rose that it was all Amelie's idea and that she was the one who forced me to do the hypnosis. I told him about the books she'd read and the chanting words, and the special foods, and the fact that she wasn't really doing her homework at all. But one glance at Amelie's confused expression was enough for him to dismiss my claims entirely.

As I walked out of his office, I could hear them talking about me.

"She's your friend Amelie. Try to be understanding," Dr. Rose said from behind the closed door. He continued with some words that were muffled but there was no mistaking that Amelie said the word "freak", which saddened me. I thought she was my friend.

That evening, I found Flynn in the den comparing old photos he'd picked up on the corner chair. He put them down slowly on the table; the faces of people I didn't know looked back at me. For a minute, I wished I had been a part of that happy family of four. They even had a dog.

"I'm sorry for what you're going through," Flynn said.

"I'll live," I replied.

If it wasn't enough that my whole family thought I was crazy, now I'd really have no friends left either.

"No, really. I believe you," he said, pointing to the photographs. "Look, in the background."

The pictures were distorted. It was hard to make out anything besides the people. And I couldn't tell where it was taken.

"The dog?" I said. "I don't get it."

"Amelie told us you said Surritz was surrounded on all sides by water, right? It's hard to see because it's in black and white, but look at the background."

Behind the smiling family was…water? It was fuzzy but it did resemble the ocean. I looked at the ground, the flowers, the clothing. Nothing seemed unusual, but there definitely was water in the print.

"Where did your family get these photographs?" Flynn asked.

My eyes darted around the room for an answer. "I really don't know."

I didn't. I knew Mama collected photographs, but I just assumed they were from family.

"I know you've felt alone, but it's only because you don't let anyone else in," Flynn said. "I can help you figure this out. I do believe your dreams might be meaningful."

I felt him staring deep into my eyes.

"We shared so much in Puncchit, but now you are drifting away," he said.

"It's not as straightforward as it seems," I answered. What could I possible tell him about Surritz that he would understand? How could I explain to him that I lived with Wayters in my past life?

He reached out and put his hand on top of mine. It was warm and soft.

"I know you. Why won't you trust me with what you're going through? I know you think Amelie has betrayed you. That we all have."

Amelie's words stung me again. *Freak*.

"You really think someone who believes in ghosts and contacting the dead doesn't believe a word you're saying?" he continued.

"I don't understand, Flynn. Amelie confessed in front of her dad today that she doesn't believe a word I'm saying. All that weird stuff she was doing with the Ouija board, it was just for fun, like we all said."

I caught myself blushing. I really hadn't talked about this with anyone besides Amelie. Flynn would never understand. How could he?

"Try me," he said as if he were reading my mind. "When Amelie was here the other day, I heard her talking to her dad on the phone. She was shouting. They were fighting."

"About what?"

"I tried not to listen but she didn't seem to care. She was here, in the den, and… and she was crying."

Amelie crying? I'd thought she was built without that gene.

I glanced out the window, confused, and Flynn continued.

"I think her dad was trying to convince her not to encourage you. She said something about age regression, that you were able to do it, and then the Ouija board, she believed you could contact…" He trailed off. "Are you listening?"

I couldn't believe Flynn had heard her talking about our hypnosis. For a selfish moment, I cared more about Flynn finding out about Nina then I did about her crying.

"We did age regression hypnosis. You're probably so confused right now. How can I ever explain to you who Nina is? You're going to really think I'm crazy," I said.

But all he answered was, "Who's Nina?"

"She didn't tell you about that? About what happened in the hypnosis?"

"No, she said she wanted us to play the Ouija board because she believed you could contact her mother."

"She was crying for her mother?"

"She said she has tried age regression many times before and it never worked, but the first time she tried it on you, you remembered strange things. She believed you could contact spirits with the Ouija board. She kept yelling 'yes she can' and it sounded like she was trying to convince him of something."

The detective in me poked her head out from underneath the covers. Amelie was crying for her mother. Why had I not been more sympathetic?

"Her mother died five years ago," I told Flynn, "and it was tragic, but we were young."

"Stasia, the point I'm trying to make is that even

though Amelie says she doesn't believe you, deep down she really does. She's just trying to hide her own insecurities from her dad."

This was all just a plot on Amelie's part to reconnect with her mother? Did she really believe it was possible? Had she tried hypnosis on others?

"You really do believe me?" I asked Flynn.

"As much as I can reach out and touch your arm right now," he said before wrapping his hand around my wrist. His warmth was comforting. It was the first time Flynn had ever touched me in a sympathetic embrace. Today was the first time he'd ever touched me at all. But now all I could think about was Amelie's mother.

"I want to help you," he finally said. "And just so you know, I *wasn't* moving the pointer in the Ouija game. I didn't even know about Billy. And now that you mention it, who's Nina?"

I spent the next two hours explaining everything down to the way Nina heard Toro speak. I actually did feel better. Several times I thought Flynn would run out of the room and get on the next plane to Puncchit, but surprisingly, he was very understanding. Despite a couple jokes at my expense, like:

"At least you have somewhere to go when it's cold."

"You said long dark hair and blue eyes – can I meet her please?"

"I don't have a tree to help me remember so don't fault me."

"Can you try to befriend the Wayters so they don't kill us?"

He really did believe me. He stared at me and gently smiled. His bangs hung over his forehead and he kept sweeping them away. I was so caught up in the moment, and his beauty, that I leaned in closer to his face. I could feel his breath on my nose.

"You want to kiss me Stasia Forrester?"

"I don't know," I said turning so red I felt like one of Mama's pies, right out of the oven. "I mean, do you?"

He leaned in more and I felt his soft lips on mine. His bangs brushed against my cheek and he touched my face with his fingers.

"So, do you really believe me, or is this all you wanted?" I asked, unable to see his eyes.

"Hey, you leaned in first. Were you just trying to impress *me* with that story, or is it true?"

We both burst out laughing before I wrapped my arms around his neck, holding on, holding on so tight I never wanted to let go.

* * *

THE NEXT night, Billy came to visit me again in St. Michael. We met quietly on the terrace below my bedroom window. Strangely, I was able to see him clearer now.

"Of course no one will believe you. Just listen to yourself," he scowled.

"I've never been a liar," I answered.

He continued to scold me for talking about Surritz.

"Because then everyone will go there?" I asked.

"You have to be a very highly developed individual to see Surritz by holding the magical stones. Everyone has lived hundreds of lives on Earth before they advance to living in Surritz. If you have not lived in Surritz before, it is impossible to experience it until you are born in that lifetime."

He moved his paws in the snow, creating the footprints I had become so familiar with. I guess it was true that people from Surritz did feel really uncomfortable without the water surrounding them. I could feel him breathe heavier now like he was anxious.

"That's why we were so confused and could not find you because somehow you ended up back on Earth after your life as Nina ended," he said.

I wanted to tell Billy what I had discovered under the Tree of Waking Thoughts. This was the perfect opportunity.

"Stasia," Mama opened up the door and startled me. "Are you talking to someone?"

I shook the shock off my face and pulled my jacket tighter. "No, just myself," I said quickly, waiting for her to go back inside so I could continue talking with Billy. Instead, she stood still.

"We will figure it out. I'm willing to listen. I don't want you to feel alone." She touched my shoulder before hugging me. Was she one of the monsters?

"But, there is something strange that I want to talk to you about. Let's go inside," she said as we walked into the kitchen.

"What?" I asked expecting her to say that the weather was getting colder, or that Pa was not selling as many Brooderkaas. Maybe Amelie's father wanted to do more research on me or I had failed my dragon classes in Puncchit.

"Maisy said that she used to have an imaginary friend too."

"Ok, Mama. I don't feel alone. I get it."

She shook her head, "The strange part is that his name was the same as your imaginary friend."

My eyes shot up to her red lips. I saw them moving

slowly but all I heard her say was, "Abe Carlton."

CHAPTER 16

MAMA LAUGHED like it was nothing.

"That's really weird. Maybe she was just joking?" I said to her.

"You probably mentioned it to her and she's just confusing names," Mama said happily before turning her head to the living room as the phone rang. But I figured *she* had probably mentioned Abe's name to Maisy, just as she did to Dr. Rose.

We both glanced at the clock. It was 10:21 PM. She slid her hand across my shoulder before running to pick up the phone receiver.

"Be right back," she called to me from the other room.

"Hello?" I heard her say as the old phone handle clicked open.

There was silence for a while before the tone in her voice changed.

"Well, are you sure? Where would she go?"

More silence.

"No, Stasia is right here. She's not with us." A pause,

then, "Yes, yes definitely. I will ask her."

The phone clicked shut and I turned around, pretending I was looking in the cabinet, which of course was empty.

"Everything okay?" I asked as she came back into the kitchen.

Her face had gone ghostly pale. "That was Dr. Rose. He said Amelie is missing. You haven't seen her, have you?"

Did I take her to Surritz? No. When did I see her last?

"She was there yesterday when I was talking to Dr. Rose, remember?"

"She never leaves the house unless she's coming here. He's really worried."

I tried to find some comforting words for Mama but nothing helped. I was scared, but it was silly; no one could have kidnapped her. They couldn't even get to the house in this weather.

"Where's Maisy?" I asked, somehow thinking they might be together.

"She's sleeping honey. In the morning, let's help Dr. Rose search the neighborhood for Amelie if she's not found by then." She didn't seem so worried anymore. "I'm sure she is playing in the basement again. I'm going to call him back and tell him to check."

MORNING CAME quickly. I had hoped that Amelie had come home, but my fear returned as I saw Mama, Pa, Flynn, and Maisy dashing around downstairs putting on layers of clothing, scarves, and hats. All their eyes were on me as I entered.

"What's going on?" I asked. Maisy glared at me. I was dying to find out what she knew about Abe.

"You ready?" Mama interrupted the stare down.

"I don't understand where Amelie would go," I said.

"She did say she was getting tired of her father," said Maisy.

"Still doesn't make sense. The only place she would have gone is here. I don't understand what she's thinking," I repeated.

I started to gather my colorless clothing: a black coat and gray boots.

"Should be easy to spot Amelie if she's outside. She only wears bright colors," said Flynn, who seemed to be reading my mind again.

"She wouldn't be outside all night, Flynn," Maisy scoffed.

Pa was preparing hot tea in the kitchen. "Mayleen, where are the thermoses?"

Pots and pans clanked together until one landed on the floor.

"Be careful," Mama hissed. "They're in the closet." She walked into the other room to retrieve them.

Everyone was on edge.

"Ready?" she asked upon returning, as she handed us our thermoses before we filed out the door.

Outside, the wind stung my face and my ears started to burn as we stepped into the slushy snow. The wind chime shook, sounding like hands beating down on a drum.

"We should check the neighbors' houses first," said Mama, walking out the gate.

"Why would she go there?" I asked.

Flynn and Maisy followed closely behind me without saying a word.

"She knows Charles Benidan and Mr. Gordon. We

can at least ask if they saw her."

"Can't we just call?" I muttered just loud enough for Mama to whip around and roll her lips together.

She was getting more and more angry. I could tell by her tone and the way her mouth twitched. She fought the urge to shout. I refrained from adding the comment about Mr. Gordon's appearance. We were worried about Amelie, but all I could think about was how old he looked. Why couldn't I focus? Maybe it was because I didn't fully believe Amelie was "missing." She wasn't stupid and she wouldn't have left home if she'd had nowhere to go.

Charles Benidan shrugged when we told him Amelie was missing. "Who?" he asked, his mustache curling downwards towards his lips.

He was another weird character. He claimed to be a professional soccer player, but I had never seen him playing the sport. I wondered how he kept his family afloat with such a profession.

"How's soccer?" I asked, my eyes on his crooked facial hair.

"It's a pastime now Stasia, with the weather and all," he replied, but I knew from Pa's slight shake of the head that I'd made him uncomfortable so I dropped it.

"Would you like to come in? Can I make you some coffee?" he asked.

"No, Charles, but thank you. We brought hot tea with us," said Pa, lifting his thermos.

"Will you let us know if you hear or see anything?" Mama asked.

"Yes, of course," he replied. "Dr. Rose's daughter. I remember now. I really haven't seen her in years."

It was cold. I was dying to go inside but Mama said

we needed to keep looking so we politely declined his invitation.

"Soccer?" Flynn asked me as we left.

"He *claims* he was making money playing soccer. Isn't that weird? There's not even a proper field here."

"Maybe he's making magic in his basement," said Flynn sarcastically. "You're so suspicious."

"How can I not be," I said to him, "after every-thing…?"

I gave him a 'remember what I told you' look and he hugged me gently, but not nearly as much as I wanted him to.

"You're buying Stasia's story also?" Maisy asked, although we hadn't realized she was listening. She chuckled as she continued walking.

Mr. Gordon provided no answers for us either. He was smoking a cigar again as he answered the door. He told us to check around the beach bar area.

"Lots of kids hanging out in there. Even breaking in and drinking," he said angrily.

"Oh Amelie would never do that, Mr. Gordon," Mama felt the need to reassure him, which Pa confirmed.

"Well I do hope she turns up then," Mr. Gordon said as we left.

The wind howled in the distance and I could hear the ocean waves crashing loudly onto the shore. I knew we were all tired of walking.

"Let's split up," Pa said taking charge, "I'll go with Flynn up the hill towards the other houses."

I wanted to go with Flynn, but when I glanced at him he nodded at me signaling that I should agree with Pa.

Pa motioned to Mama next, "Mayleen, you take the girls down towards the water."

Before I could get a word in, they were disappearing into the heavy snow and fog. I saw Pa's red jacket far in the distance but could not make out anything else. He did not even say when we were meeting, where we were meeting, and how we could get a hold of each other.

As we shuffled down the snowy hill, I unintentionally blurted out something I'd hoped would stay in my mind. I told Mama I knew where Amelie was.

Or at least I thought I did.

"Why didn't you say something before?" she asked.

"I just put the pieces together."

She stood in the snow motionless like a snowman, or better yet, one of the tree stumps.

If Amelie had really believed all that I was saying, she was sure to try to go to Surritz.

"Follow me," I said as I kept walking, giving them no chance to abandon me now. Maisy huffed and puffed for a while, purposely falling behind and claiming it was too cold to continue.

"This is ridiculous. There's too much snow," she complained.

"Is this the imaginary place again?" Mama asked.

I wasn't quick enough to make up an excuse. If I had been with Flynn, I know he would have backed me up.

"I told Amelie all about my dreams of Surritz. I know she is trying to go there," I said.

Maisy rolled her eyes. "How would she go to a place you're dreaming about? It's only a dream."

"Because I went there the other day, when I left at night to look for the footprints. I think she knows that. She's been hiding her intentions about everything this whole time!"

Mama stopped walking and looked at me like I was

crazy. But I pushed on; I needed to get Mama to the beach. I needed to know whether Mama had lived in Surritz before. According to Billy, if she did, she'd be able to see the magical beach when she held one of the gems.

Images of Billy, Nina, Amelie, and Maisy all mixed together in my head. The wind danced around me and my head beat harder than my heart. Scenes flashed into my mind making it hard to differentiate reality from past life and the dream world.

I reached out to pull Mama's hand, hoping she'd walk a little faster.

"Stasia, this place better be close. I can't take much more of this weather and your stories."

"Only a few more steps," I looked around my feet, hoping to find a gem.

The snow was thick and I couldn't see anything radiating on the ground. Dropping to my hands and knees as if I was about to pray, I dug. The icy snow cut through my hands like a bear trap. I started to crawl through the snow, pushing ice and grass out of my way, determined to find one. When I was just about to stop, there it was shining through the snow like it had been waiting for me for years.

"It's here. I found it!" I picked up a ruby and held it tightly in my right palm. The warmth made all the icy pain diminish. My hands tingled as if I had them right above a warm fire. I closed my eyes and saw myself sitting comfortably in a little log cabin, roasting chestnuts and singing old songs. I tuned out St. Michael completely. I actually felt like I *was* in this house!

It was only when Maisy yanked my arm backwards that I opened my eyes to see another pleasant scene. The beach. There it was. The light blue ocean dazzled, inviting me to swim inside. I stepped over onto the white sand that melted through my toes. Lifting my face towards the sky I felt the sun's rays penetrate deep within my skin.

When I looked back happily, I saw my Mama shivering.

"Let's go back!" Her voice shot through my body, jolting me back to reality.

I held out my hand for her to take the stone.
She ignored me and was turning around until she saw the ruby sparkle.

"Where did you find that?"

"On the ground." I lifted up my palm.

"It's cold. Let's go Stasia," said Maisy. "Please."

I lifted my hand again and felt Mama's icy fingers brush my warm hands. She gripped the ruby with two fingers, looking at it and then peering towards the ocean.

"Can you see it?" I asked.

Several moments passed. "See what? See what, Stasia! What is going on with you?" She was so angry she was about to toss it on the ground before Maisy reached out and took it.

She rubbed it with her index finger and thumb. "I don't see anything either."

But she stood up straight, took her hands out of her pockets and titled her head towards the sun. She stopped shivering. She felt the warm beach.

"See Mrs. Forrester, I told you," Maisy said.

"Told you what?" I asked angrily.

"You're imagining everything," Mama said, too irritated to be concerned now. "This is not funny."

"Let's just go back," said Maisy.

The snow started to blow around and icy particles stung my eyes. Mama, who was always so careful with her expressions and my fragility, shook her head with anger. They both turned around and started to walk back through the woods. I waited a few minutes staring at their bodies slowly moving through the snow like they were survivors in an avalanche.

When I could barely see them anymore I yelled, "I know where Amelie is. She's in Surritz. I'm going there to find her. I'm going now!"

Neither turned around, their movement still slow but steady.

* * *

WHEN I got to Surritz, Billy took me to the only house that had a fire roaring and smoke lifting from the chimney. Inside, it cracked and spit out of the fireplace. It was the most heat I had felt in weeks. This was the first time I was in Surritz at night. It was quiet and the warm breeze reminded me of the days when St. Michael was still hot. The only difference was that life had diminished in Surritz. No animal sounds broke the night's silence.

We sat on the porch and with the foggy night, the only light I could see was the little candle Billy placed on the outside table.

"Is it true? Wayters are coming to live in St. Michael? Perhaps to eat us?"

Billy's nostrils flared and his tongue slipped out of his mouth like a lizard's.

"Where would you have heard such a preposterous thing?" he asked, folding his two front paws together. His claws were long and slender, but the rest of his paws looked humanlike. "We don't *eat* anything."

"What do you mean you don't eat?"

"Wayters get all their energy from heat. Mainly the sun and fire from the volcano. That's why we used to hang out at the peak. We basked in the lava. We also absorb the sunlight in the water as we swim."

"I don't understand. Wayters are supposed to come ashore to hunt for more food."

"Wayters are coming ashore, but not for those reasons. We need to be closer to the sun. The universe is getting colder. We haven't been able to get enough energy from our volcano, which has been inactive for years. It has turned into a waterfall."

He switched his attention to the door as it opened.

"Stasia, this is Fabienne," he said as an older woman walked out of the house. Fabienne placed two cups of tea on the table in front of me. Her eyes stayed fixated on mine.

"Nice to meet you," she said quietly.

"I'm looking for Amelie. Have you seen her?" I asked them. "She's a friend. I think she might be here."

She and Billy both shook their heads in unison. I felt guilty for leaving Mama and Maisy to come back to Surritz. They were probably still searching around St. Michael for Amelie. I wondered if they met up with Pa and Flynn again. What would Mama tell Pa about where I went? *He's going to be so angry*, I thought. If only they believed me. I was certain Amelie had come here.

"I really have to find her. I never paid attention to what she needed," I said to Billy and Fabienne.

"Stasia, I have to be on my way. If I see her I'll let you know," Billy said abruptly, then left.

Fabienne's feet shuffled on the wooden floor. "Not too many visitors coming through here. I doubt you will find your friend in Surritz."

"I have to try." But as I said the words, I didn't even know where to start.

"Don't you see? There's hardly any life left in Surritz. If someone new were to come, we would have known. Not too many thoughts floating around these days."

"Thoughts of what?"

"Thoughts of energy. Every time you think something, more energy is released. Since there are barely any people, and no animals, the air is clear."

"Why are there no animals? I remembered so many in my lifetime here."

Fabienne had bright pink energy coming from her body. Every sip of the tea enhanced the deepness. It felt good. Familiar. I liked her presence.

"There were many animals during your time in Surritz. Hundreds," she said reluctantly.

"What happened?"

She drank another sip. "Right after you were killed, animals started to die. Kill themselves. So many that all we have left is the ocean life and the dragons. You, or Nina I should say, had a special connection with animals."

I breathed in the warm steam of my chamomile tea as I remembered Nina's last thought.
I hear Toro speak.

"Let me take you to the Tree of Waking Thoughts. I will give you the branch that will take you back in time to the moment you are asking about," Fabienne said.

"What about Amelie?" I asked, "I need to take care of her first."

"I will look for her while you are there. Is that okay? If I find her or hear any word about her, I will wake you."

She held out her hand to take mine. It was old and fragile; wrinkles formed rings around her knuckles. When her hand fit perfectly in mine, I felt so comfortable with her that I didn't bother to refuse. I trusted her.

The Tree of Waking Thoughts had many, many different colors that radiated from it. I recognized the pink to be the same one that radiated from Fabienne. Each branch was different. Fabienne grabbed the one that was yellow and handed it to me.

"You rest now. I'll see you later," she said, as she helped me into the tree trunk.

I immediately felt tired. For the first time since I discovered Surritz, I wondered if I'd ever go home to St. Michael again. The images of Nina, Abe, Toro, and all the animals flashed through my mind until suddenly I was looking at Surritz as Nina again.

CHAPTER 17

THE FIRST time I heard Toro speak was the closest I have ever felt to witnessing a miracle. "Master! Can it be?" Toro said the day he was reunited with Abe.

Master. The word repeats in my mind. *Master.*

His words were clear and crisp. It was not like a baby learning to speak, but like a man who had mastered his craft of the human language. I was far away on the hill, and the wind was blowing, but I definitely heard it. *Master!*

Things went back to normal after that day. For Abe at least. I didn't tell him what I heard. I only watched as he and Toro hugged and all the animals surrounded them as if for protection. I was glad I was off the hook for losing Toro. There would definitely be no more hugs between Abe and me if Toro had died. Abe went back to his rituals of feeding the animals in the barn every day, going to school in the afternoon, and then heading back into the woods.

But something was different for me. I heard them talking. It was not just Toro and Abe, although they were the first. I heard Abe communicating with *all* the animals. Toro told him that he didn't like me and that I abandoned him after Abe left. He told him the whole story about how he ran into the woods only to have me call a few times but not bother to follow. He said he did it to test me in order to see how loyal I was to Abe.

I knew he was trying to get between us. But I sat with Abe in the barn while he fed everyone and pretended that I didn't hear anything. Abe felt completely comfortable talking to the animals; he was completely confident that there was no way I could hear anything. I now understood why animals look up at people with their big, round, sad eyes. It is because they are being cheeky, talking about us.

That was the expression on Toro as he talked about me. He kept glancing up to stare. Another human observer would say, "Aw what a cute dragon." But to me, I heard his words, "That girl is just trouble you see, Abe."

Abe continued petting him, smiling. To his credit, he never took Toro's words to heart.

I knew that no one else in Surritz could understand the animals. If they could, they would have reacted to the conversations. Animals talking to humans, talking about humans, talking about other animals! There's no way anyone could suspect it.

So what is going on? Am I daydreaming? I want to ask Abe today when I see him in the barn. I have wanted to ask him since the day it started, but I am having too much fun listening in on all their conversations.

It is 9 AM and I take the walk through the woods, which I am no longer scared to enter. Hearing the thoughts of all the animals has definitely helped me to remain calm when I encounter them. The scariest ones—big cats, bears, and surprisingly, the small orange monkeys—are actually pretty pure in thought.

Not prey. Just another human. They say as I pass.

So they don't want to attack me after all.

It is a beautiful day and the sun peeks through the foliage, lighting up the fallen leaves. They crack underneath my feet and I can feel the cool sensation of mud soak through my shoes.

When I enter around the back of the castle into the herb garden, I hear Abe's voice. It is so pleasant. So confident. And then I recognize the voice of the creature he is talking to. It's Belli, the blue lion cat. For a minute I hide to eavesdrop, and then I remember that they don't know that I can hear them. I walk around the corner, give them a quick wave so as not to interrupt their train of thought, and continue picking chives not far away.

"Are you in love with her?" Belli asks.

"I don't know. It just happened so fast," Abe answers.

I can feel myself turning red. I want to look at him but I am overcome with the flushing sensation on my face.

"How will you ever tell her?" Belli asks.

"I guess she will never know," Abe answers.

"I'm sure there's a way."

"Maybe. But obviously I just can't pursue it, can I?" Abe says before he catches me staring.

"Herbs have grown three inches overnight!" I say to him. "You want to try these chives. So fresh and delicious. So…green."

I am blabbing, but he doesn't seem to suspect anything. His hair has fallen around his face in those soft waves that I love. His skin is a silky, tan color with a little pink on his cheeks. His clean white t-shirt hangs perfectly from his body. I had been denying my feelings for him the whole time, but now I feel confident. I feel, love.

CHAPTER 18

THE MORNING passes, but Abe doesn't speak about his feelings for me again. There's small chatter going on with the animals, but nothing interesting. School is canceled because this afternoon there is going to be another town meeting, which Abe is dreading because he doesn't like being the center of attention.

Ding, Ding, Dong. The bell rings and we hear it all the way in the corner of the woods.

"Well, here we go again," he says uncomfortably.

"Will you tell them today, about the monsters?" I ask.

"I can't tell everyone that, Nina. What would they think? I don't want to start a panic. If everyone knew about the people in St. Michael, it would scare them half to death. I already have people asking me if I think the people from Earth can come to Surritz."

"Do you?" I ask.

I can tell he doesn't feel like talking about it and I wonder why the subject is sore with him.

"I doubt it. If they could, they would have. They have poked around at every resource on their land. I'm sure if they could come here, they would have found the way already."

As we walk through the woods and along the ocean side, needlefish swim along with us, sticking their tails in and out of the water. When we are almost in town, a big, green tail blocks our way like a gate.

"Oh, it's Elgor!" Abe says before I notice the Wayter that brought him back from St. Michael. Elgor swings around in less than a second and sticks his nose out of the water. They begin a conversation immediately as I watch.

"How is she?" Abe asks him.

"I haven't seen her. She used to come to the beach all the time. Since you left, she hasn't been there."

Abe seems worried and disappointed.

"Good boy," Abe says out loud as he glides his hand over the dragon's head. He is very careful not to stop too long, in order for me not to suspect anything.

What is going on? I scream in my head, igniting thoughts of confusion and jealousy.

At that moment, Elgor swings his head to the side to face me. I swear that I see a change in his expression.

You do hear me! I think again and the dragon says, "Yes."

"Yes what?" Abe asks.

"Nothing," Elgor responds.

Why didn't he tell Abe?

"We should get going, Abe. Don't want you to be late for your own press conference," I say.

Elgor doesn't take his eyes off me. Abe says goodbye to him and tells him to check in with him to let him know the "status."

At that point, I want to tell Abe that I hear everything he is saying. I am mad that he is having conversations behind my back. Why didn't he tell me his secret? And what girl was he talking about?

The bell tolls again in the town square. It rings faster now, forcing us to run until we are out of the woods.

"Really not looking forward to this," Abe says, out of breath.

I can't help but be upset at what just happened. He notices my mood, but doesn't ask about it.

Just about everyone on the island has gathered in the town. I haven't seen it this busy since Abe's return.

"What do they want to ask you now?" I say, before anyone notices him and the bombarding begins.

"Who knows," he answers.

This time, the blankets are more structured. They are neatly lined up, ten towels per row, and all the same color, so I assume that the officials have planned the event. No one is being rowdy. No one is excited. People sit in their chairs and I wonder what the news is about. The ocean becomes murky and fog rolls in. To my surprise, when people notice me and Abe walking into the town, they do not get up.

When I see my aunt, uncle, and sister Fabienne on our green towel, I tell Abe that I will meet up with him later. He agrees and we part ways.

"Do you know what is going on?" I ask Fabienne.

"Do you?" my uncle responds curiously.

"No," I reply.

My aunt has the same look that she had when I returned with Bisket before he died.

"The meeting was called last minute," my uncle says as he holds my aunt's hand.

"Well, I suspect something to do with Abe," I say.

"Oh, definitely," says Fabienne. "They already told us

that."

The images of the monsters in my dreams race through my mind again. They are marching towards me. They each wear three pairs of shoes, one on top of the next. The women have neatly pressed curls on their heads, and the men are so nicely shaven that they look like young boys.

"Oh, there they are. They are about to begin," says my uncle, pointing to the officials.

Cornelius, the one in charge, speaks. "We have received another note in a bottle."

People gasp and I know that they have not received this information previously. I shift my gaze frantically looking for Abe, but I have lost sight of him.

"I'm going to read to you all what it says. Anyone with any information should come forward as we are trying to figure out its meaning. Please don't be alarmed and don't jump to conclusions," says Cornelius.

He pulls out a rather large bottle with a long slender top. Obviously they already read the note, so I wonder why they put it back in the bottle. For effect, I assume.

He reaches into the bottle with a set of long tweezers. The note is unrolled as he clears his throat before speaking.

"Dear Arlo,
I don't know where you are or where you have gone. One minute you were here and then it was like I awoke from a dream. I know you will never receive this letter, but I am putting it out there, into the universe. If it's fate, it will find its way to you. Arlo, I just found out, and I have not told anyone else… I am having a child. And it's yours."

"That is all," says Cornelius as he snaps the paper shut in his palm, "And there was no signature. I am hoping

Abe can give us some insight into whether he has met Arlo. Who is this man and why has this bottle found its way to Surritz?"

I finally spot Abe sitting in the front row. He gets up quickly to address the awaiting crowd and their expressionless faces. The mood of the audience is now one of suspicion. What were these people told to make them believe that Abe is involved? When he says that he doesn't know who Arlo is, people sink down into their towels.

"I can only tell you that Earth is such a large place. It's not like Surritz. Imagine one thousand places like Surritz all making up one Earth. This guy, he could be anyone. And that is all I have to say." Abe throws his hands into his pockets as he walks away from the platform.

I can't help but think that Abe knows more than he is revealing. Why did he lie about the way he found the funnel? The question nags at me constantly. Did he know about Earth before? Was he in some way connected to it before he even left? I didn't know Abe well enough to come to my own conclusions, but I really wanted to believe what he told me.

"Maybe there is a connection with the diamond?" asks Cornelius.

This time, people are not allowed to scream out to Abe. Cornelius handles the whole thing very well. He even dressed up again for the occasion, looking very formal in his black shirt and matching leather shoes.

"I've told you all I know about the diamond, I really have," finishes Abe.

CHAPTER 19

WHEN ABE leaves the makeshift stage, it is clear that people don't believe what he said. There is chatter in the air. No one is excited to see him, like they were for his return from Earth. Surprisingly, Abe returns to the blanket I share with my family, instead of going back to his own. After greeting Fabienne, Aunt Agnes, and Uncle Pete, he says that he wants to leave and asks if I will accompany him. There is no hesitation on my end.

"Abe, is it true you don't know anything about Arlo?" asks my uncle uncontrollably before we leave.

"No, sir," responds Abe politely.

"But, what about—" my uncle begins his interrogations, unable to help his curiosity.

"About what? Can't you just leave him alone," I say, coming to Abe's defense before grabbing his arm. "Let's go."

We quickly whisk away and begin the trek out of the town. As we approach the forest, many animals peek out of the bushes and follow us. Abe is clearly aware of their presence, but he does not have any conversations with them. When I cannot take any more of his strange behavior, I stop him in his tracks and demand his attention.

"Why did you lie about how you found the funnel? I was there; it was a surprise to the both of us," I say. "Did you know about it before?"

"You'd never believe me if I told you," he quickly answers, surely having anticipated my question for days.

"I want you to trust me. I believe you. I'm on your side," I say. I grab his hand tightly, although he does not reciprocate.

"Let's go to the lake. I will tell you there," he says.

It's not far away. We walk in silence until the water comes into view through the trees. There is sorrow in Abe's face. Wrinkles are forming around his mouth. His eyes droop. He doesn't say anything, even after we sit down.

After taking off his shoes, Abe's feet dangle in the water. It's so clear that we can see to the bottom where stingrays rest. Needlefish gather around us.

"They're hungry," says Abe.

I already know because I hear them too.

But it isn't the fish that I am interested in at this time. Instead, it's the colors. Bright reds, pinks, yellows, oranges, and purples stream off his toes. The needlefish swim away quickly, jumping and spinning like they can't wait to catch the colors.

I have never seen anything like this before.

"What is that?" I ask him.

"It's energy," he replies. "I know how to release it from my body. It happens naturally."

He continues to explain that he never knew what it was until Toro noticed it one day.

"He told me what it means," says Abe. "Yeah, *told* me."

Although I already know what he is going to tell me, I play dumb.

"I have a talent, Nina. It's why I told you Toro was so important to me. He made me realize what it is."

"What did he make you realize?" I ask.

He becomes fidgety. Does he think I will judge him? Not believe him?

He tells me the story.

Toro saw the colors in the water one day, and it was after that moment that he tried to communicate with Abe. Abe was surprised when he heard Toro. He could understand everything Toro was saying. The colors, Toro said, are what every animal possesses. It's energy that flows through them and continues on to the next animal. It's what provides the animals with instincts and reflexes. It is knowledge being passed on from one being to another. Humans don't have that capability because they hold on to energy, essentially hoarding it and not releasing it back into the universe. This prevents the flow of information to one another. Animals understand each other; they always have. It's all about awareness. And once Abe became aware, he found out he could communicate with all animals.

When Abe is done explaining something that I don't really understand, I ask him again why he lied about the funnel.

"Toro told me about it," he says. "I don't know how he knew, but he told me to go there, that I would be able to travel to another land. I didn't believe him. That's why I didn't tell you. I don't want you to think I am hiding something from you. But by the time I launched through the funnel, I couldn't take you with me or else I would have."

He reaches out to grab my hand and I melt at the

feeling of it. I'm glad he finally told me the truth.

"When was it that Toro made you realize you could speak to animals?" I ask, gripping his hand so hard that even mine hurt.

"I was five," says Abe. "I remember hearing animal's thoughts; I just always thought it was normal."

"Is that why you always feed them now?" I say.

"Yes, it was only natural what my role would become," answers Abe.

"Your role?"

"I am the Master of Animals," he says quietly.

CHAPTER 20

WHEN I questioned Abe about his duties, he only answered, "I'm facilitating the never ending development of their souls." But why did the animals need a master? What did they do before Abe was around?

It's the middle of the night when I wake up to these questions rolling around in my head. The ceiling fan is spinning quickly but I can't seem to get cool enough. Sweat gathers on the arch of my back and my hair is sticky and bunched together on the pillow. I look to my right and hear the comforting sound of Fabienne breathing softly as she sleeps. A whistle runs through her lips, inviting me to study her features. With her dark hair and blue eyes, we look similar. But the moles on her face are absent on mine.

It isn't long before I am tossing and turning in bed again. I try counting to fifty in the hopes that I will fall back asleep. Instead, the questions keep coming back into my mind.

Why can I hear the animals?
Why is Elgor the only one who can hear me?
Should I tell Abe?

What will he think?

The heat is making me dizzy. The soft sheets are wet with sweat and I can't get comfortable.

I walk outside with no plan as to where I'm going. There are hundreds of twinkling glow fish above me. The trees are visible, casting many shadows below me. The ground is damp and cool and a constant breeze blows past me. I head towards the woods. The ability to hear the animals' thoughts has given me so much confidence, that I am even willing to walk by myself through the forest, at night no less. Even though an animal could attack me anyway, I figure that at least I will know it's coming.

It is darker once I reach the center of the dozens of trees. When I look up, I can no longer see the water or the glow fish. I decide to head to the castle. Occasionally, Abe sleeps there and I might be able to see him. A smile forms on my face as I think of him, until I hear a rustling sound in the bushes.

"What is it?" someone asks.

"A girl… his girl," says another.

I don't have night vision like most of the animals, so it's hard to see what's going on. They talk some more but I can't understand what they are saying. The breeze blows through the branches and the only noise I can hear is the sound of leaves falling to the ground.

"Let's go," says the first one.

I stay still until I see them run in front of me. Two dragons. They look like Toro, but a little smaller.

I keep walking straight ahead. I've never been lost, but I soon find that nothing seems familiar to me. The trees are larger and have a different shape than normal. I am supposed to be in the middle of the woods, but I run into the side of the ocean. I gather that I have been walking east, instead of north. The east side is the only area where the water meets the forest. The glow fish come back into view and I can see all the way up the coast.

I walk out of the forest and towards the ocean. It is still like the pond. I can see everything under the water due to the fluorescent light of the glow fish. Different colored corals dot the floor. Algae moves slowly with the current. Seaweed drifts by. Small red colored fish swim slowly in schools. The ocean floor is full of life until something sweeps by in the distance. The fish disappear before I can blink. The open shells close quickly.

Before I know it, I am staring at a water dragon. I automatically look back into the forest, wondering if I should run. But then I hear it speak.

"You hear me?" it says and I recognize him. It's Elgor, the same Wayter Abe and I were talking to yesterday.

I nod.

"I had never encountered another human that could understand me. And now it's two in the last couple years," says Elgor, excitedly.

I have seen many dragons before, but never *talking* to me!

He looks much larger than he did the day Abe returned from Earth. His light green body looks like plastic and his eyes are big and bubbly. He is intelligent. I can see that.

"This is new for me," I say.

"When I met your friend on Earth, he told me about this place. He asked me to bring him back. He didn't know how he got there."

"He was stuck there for a while," I say, laughing.

I am glad that I can laugh about it now that he is back.

"So you live up there?" I ask.

"Mostly. I like to fly in and out of the waters. Can't do that here," he says.

"You can just go back and forth like it's nothing?" I ask.

Was it really that easy? Could anyone travel between Surritz and Earth when and if they wanted? Can I get on his back right now and go there?

"Only some can. I've tried to take others here, they just hit rock bottom. It has something to do with development."

"Development of what?" I ask him.

"The consciousness of course," he says. "It comes from practice. You can't come here unless you've lived in this place before. You have to let the energy flow. Dragons are pretty highly developed animals. We're the only animals that possess reason, like humans."

"What does that mean?" I ask him.

"Animals listen, love, and learn, but they don't build. We are the only species of animals that can create. Sometimes it works against us. When some of us discover different emotions like envy and greed, we automatically gravitate towards them."

"But you seem very nice, Elgor," I say.

"All I'm saying is that Wayters are complex animals. No two are alike. We are not vicious by nature, but be careful; we are subjected to all the evils just like you are."

He turns his tail around so that it sticks out of the ocean.

"You, for instance, are very unique too. Very different

from other humans," he says.

I ask him how he knows and he tells me that most cannot communicate with animals. He never met anyone besides Arlo that can.

"Arlo?" I ask.

"What a great man," Elgor replies.

"You've met Arlo?" I say.

"I just told you, I'm the one who brought him to you, back from Earth. Aren't you happy to see him again?"

I feel dizzy again, but this time for a different reason. Abe has been lying to us the whole time.

CHAPTER 21

I NEVER make it to the castle. I'm on the ground by the ocean; my head feels like it's spinning off in a thousand different directions. I say goodbye to Elgor and he promises to look for me again.

Abe's not lying. There has to be an explanation, I think to myself.

Before I know it, the sun is beaming down on my face. It feels stiff. Burned. Salt particles are caked on my skin. My hair is knotted into tiny, long rolls.

I fell asleep. I dreamed this.

But then I remember the note:

Dear Arlo, I don't know where you are or where you have gone. One minute you were here and then it was like I awoke from a dream. I know you will never receive this letter, but I am putting it out there, into the universe. If it's fate, it will find its way to you. Arlo, I just found out, and I have not told anyone else… I am having a child. And it's yours.

Jealousy burns deep in my veins. The girl he talked about with the animals. It's not me. It's the girl on Earth. The one having his child.

When I get home, I am as red as a tomato. I slide my fingernails over the skin on my face and feel the sand peel away with every scratch.

"You missed breakfast. Where did you go now?" Fabienne asks, without looking at me.

"Out," I say, before sitting down at the table with my family.

"So where *did* you go?" my uncle asks.

"I went for a walk, to the ocean. It's so hot in this house."

I tie my hair in a knot on the top of my head and pretend to rub away the sweat on my forehead. With this gesture, my aunt gets up to open the windows a little wider.

"Abe came by," she says, picking up the plates and rinsing them in the sink.

"When?" I ask softly, as my heart pounds.

"Interested now, aren't you?" Fabienne says, but I don't bother to respond.

"He was here about half an hour ago," she says. "He said to tell you to meet him at your usual spot."

"Where's that?" my uncle asks.

"None of your business," I say, before apologizing quickly. "I'll see you later."

It takes me about five minutes to change clothes and run out the door. I debate whether or not to ask Abe what is going on. He is in love with someone on Earth. Could it be? Maybe he just pretended to be Arlo. Arlo is someone else. He is trying to get information out of Elgor. But why, then, did he not tell me he knew who Arlo was after the note was read. Why does he keep hiding everything?

I am rushing to the castle when I realize that I am so

mad that I can't fake it. A loss of control sweeps over me and I feel the tears streaming down my face. Part of me feels like I should keep it together and wipe my emotions clean. The ocean is raining above my head and the drops glide perfectly over my face, concealing my tears.

Somewhere along the way, I think back to when I never experienced emotions like this. Before I turned twelve, I never even noticed that boys lived in this world. I was more concerned with Fabienne, who constantly stole my dolls and hid them around the island.

"Don't ask me, don't ask me," she recited when I questioned where they were. At that age, I truly believed that I loved those dolls, and it was a painful feeling to lose them. But not like this. Upon entering adulthood, loving inanimate objects seemed so trivial.

Before arriving at the castle, I slow down to spend some time in the forest. The conversations have gotten louder and louder, and more frequent. Birds in the trees talk about how great it is to be fed by the people, goats are challenging each other to games, and dragons speak of a diamond.

The diamond Abe brought back!

"You think it really is as he says?" one asks.

"It brings happiness," says the other.

"I heard it can cure illnesses," says the third.

They form a circle in the bush, speaking loudly until the first one spots me. They all look up in unison. I smile and pretend to walk the other way.

"What are you worried about?" says the first. "She can't hear us anyway."

They all laugh. I glance back out of spite, but this time they don't notice.

"We have to get a little feel of it, just to see. It could change our lives," says the third.

The second one scoffs, "You'll never get it from him. He said it will never leave his sight."

"Well that's easy; it must be with him then."

"You know what to do."

"Sure do."

I hear them in the background, but I am far away now. My mind wanders back to the woman that Abe loves, and all I can see are the monsters in my dreams. Angry, big ladies walking towards me with their jewels and expensive clothing, their hair braided in fancy strands, and their toenails painted different colors.

If that is what he likes, I just want to be one of them.

CHAPTER 22

WHEN I reach the castle to ask Abe about the lady he really loves, he is already waiting for me. I squint my eyes, and a smile barely breaks on my face. My posture is erect and I can't help but stand unusually far away from him. He is sitting in the same living room with the small fireplace.

It took me a while to pass all the animals when I was looking for him. This time, I got the sense that they could understand me. None of them engaged in conversation but all of them were focused on my every step. As I made my way back through the tunnels, fear crept up in the back of my mind.

Abe greets me with only a quick hello, before informing me that we need to talk.

I want to know the truth, but the answers frighten me. If it's not something that I would like, I don't want to hear it at all. I want to love him. I want him all for myself, to live happily ever after.

I sit down on the large green sofa, afraid to look into his eyes before he speaks.

"I have to tell you something, about St. Michael," he

says.

All I can think about is the beautiful monster who captured Abe's heart. With her colorful necklaces, perfect clothes, and manicured nails, there's no way I can compete.

"Are you listening?" he asks. "I just said the note the woman sent to Arlo… it was for me. I am Arlo."

"You're not the only one with these talents," I say, looking directly at him.

When I expect him to be surprised, he quietly explains that he already knows that I am learning to communicate with the animals. He says he has known from the beginning.

"What are you talking about?" I ask.

"When we met, I could feel that you had something that could be developed," he says. "I just didn't know when it was going to happen."

I assume the animals told him. Elgor. The dragons. All the conversations I have heard. Could they really hear me too?

"What did you want to tell me about St. Michael, and why did you lie about who you were?"

"I didn't lie."

"So are you Abe or are you Arlo?"

The thought of losing Abe to one of the monsters drives me crazy. I'm afraid he will tell me that he wants to go back to St. Michael. But instead, he explains that he made up the name Arlo to prevent anyone in St. Michael from discovering his real identity. Not that he thought they could, but he didn't know for sure.

A storm develops outside and both of us sit quietly for what seems like half an hour. The wind whistles through the trees and the ocean drops large pockets of water on the roof.

"So you love her?" I say, more calmly now.

"She's not a monster, Nina. They are not all as I explained to you before."

"Would you have come back to Surritz if you knew she was pregnant?"

"I was always planning to come back."

"So that's it. That's what you want to say?"

"No, Nina, I want to tell you what I've wanted to say for a long time."

He reaches into his pocket and pulls out the white diamond. It looks bigger than it did before. The colors that reflect from it are indescribable.

"Take it. Get rid of it. It's dangerous. I don't know what's going to happen in Surritz. I'm afraid."

"Afraid of what?" I ask. "Afraid of what, Abe?"

At that moment, he's sitting close to me, and I can feel the heat radiating from his body. I comfort him by touching his shoulder.

"What are you afraid of?" I ask again.

"I'm afraid for my life," he says as his eyes pierce into mine. "After all I've seen. The intentions. The devastation. The bad thoughts and negative energy. I just can't take it anymore, Nina. I don't know what's going to happen," he says. He puts his hand on mine, squeezing tightly. "I want you to be...to be the Lady of Animals." He holds out the diamond with two fingers.

I am puzzled. I'm at a loss for words. Is he serious?

"You're stronger than I am. You can do right with the diamond. Just, just destroy it. Don't let it show you what it has shown me," he says.

In this moment, another emotion takes over me. I

begin to heal. All of the doubt in my mind about Abe and the monsters, traveling away from Surritz, the lying, changing identities—it all suddenly seems trivial. He wants me to be the same as he. An equal. A partner.

"Nothing is going to happen to you. Nothing will," I say.

He pulls me towards him and I thrust forward, hugging him. The smell of his skin and hair make it so hard to let go.

"You don't care about the child?" I finally say, hesitantly.

"She will take care of it," he says. "She's a good lady Nina. Mayleen is a really good lady. She will be alright."

It is the first time he has said her name. Does she think he is dead? Did he just disappear? I brush those thoughts away because in this moment, with Abe in my arms, nothing else matters. Nothing will take him away again.

CHAPTER 23

THREE YEARS passed, and I performed my duties as the Lady of Animals quite well. The day after being indoctrinated, Abe took me to a special room inside the castle. I didn't even know it existed. There were dozens of animals there. Most of them sat around a square table, others were on the floor or sitting on old tree stumps. Simultaneously, they all stopped what they were doing and turned to me. Some looked at me with blank faces, some smiled, and others looked at me up and down, examining me carefully.

The animals were all playing games; some shuffled cards, others had chessboards. A goat and a fox played a game with sticks and rocks. If the goat balanced the stick on the rock, he got a point. If it fell, his stick was taken away and given to the next player. If one ran out of sticks, he was out. Simple, yet quite enjoyable.

The goat and the fox were very serious about their game. Even when I went closer to examine the board, they didn't flinch.

"The reason you are here is because every animal you see at this table is the oldest member of each species. Dr.

Sally, over there, the old brown goat, she is eighteen. Jack, the black horse at the end, he is twenty-one. Sparky, the turtle, he is ninety-eight. Juni, that spunky little parrot, she is one hundred and thirty-four! You never guessed you were in a senior citizens home, did you?" Abe's deep laugh filled the room as he titled his head back several times, chuckling to himself.

The oldest animals were the most fun to be around. They were the first ones I could clearly communicate with. They told me stories that I had never even imagined could happen. They were loving, kind, and generous.

I quickly forgot about Mayleen. I didn't care anymore about what happened to Abe in St. Michael. I was in his inner world now. I was part of something no one else in Surritz even knew about. I could pass animals on the street, in the water, or in town, have conversations with them and no human being would know what was going on. People started to think of me differently too. I knew things—things the animals told me. When people thought no one was looking, the animals were watching and they came back to the castle and we all had a good laugh about the stories they told.

One day Sparky told me about how my sister had stood up for me when some kids were calling me names. She had quickly defended me, something I never thought she'd do in a million years.

I thought about her differently from then on. I made an effort to talk to her when I returned home at the end of each day. I told her to talk to the boy she liked, because I found out through Juni that he liked her too. When she was brave enough to do it and it worked out, she couldn't thank me enough. Finally she had someone in her life; she was happy. I had to admit, I was happy too.

Abe seemed to be doing well also. When he finally got all his secrets out about St. Michael, Arlo, and Mayleen, he began to relax.

The only person that is not happy is Toro. I still don't know how he knew about the funnel to Earth. He definitely doesn't like the fact that I am the Lady of Animals.

And then there is the diamond in my pocket. I feel guilty that I haven't destroyed it, as Abe had asked me to. Has it started its magic? I am scared of it turning me into a monster. I am starting to dress differently. I care about how my hair looks and how I talk. I wear jewelry and I can't seem to stop thinking about ways that I can display the diamond to the world.

That's why I finally came to the decision to get rid of the stone. I want to hide it so no one can ever find it again. I will destroy the only trace of St. Michael that we still have.

CHAPTER 24

SOMETHING JOLTED me and I awoke underneath the Tree of Waking Thoughts in a cold sweat. As I sat up, I ran my fingers over the birthmark on my neck. My heart pounded as if it were trying to break out of my body. The cool, crisp breeze of the night touched my nose as it swiftly floated by. My head began to spin as I wondered who was watching me. Was someone following me? The unfamiliar land I stumbled upon just weeks ago had now changed into a place I knew very well. Just past the lake was Fabienne's house—my dear sister who had probably mourned for so long after my death. As I remembered the way she once was, I noticed the difference in her age. Her tender, tight skin had begun to form large wrinkles. The whites of her eyes were marked by yellow. They were smaller, sadder. I could feel how unhappy she was. Why didn't she tell me that I was her sister?

The dreaded thought that Mama may be the same woman Abe loved flashed through my mind. How many people named Mayleen were there on St. Michael anyway? Could it be possible?

No, no! It just couldn't be.

And then I remembered Amelie. Had she been found?

I had indulged in my curiosity about my past life before finding her. She could have been killed by now. My heart pounded in my chest. I took three long breaths to settle myself before I got up. At that moment, the wind picked up and a branch swayed right in front of me. It had a large, white glowing leaf that I couldn't push away from my face. Instead, I grabbed the leaf and it broke off easily, falling right into my palm. I stuffed it in my pocket, hoping I could use it to travel back in time whenever I wanted, wherever I was.

As I walked back towards the water, a dragon stopped to look at me, bewildered. I offered some comfort and told him to come closer so we could speak. But, as I reached out my hand, he scampered away.

I tried to reorient myself. My clothes were wet with sweat and my hair stuck to the sides of my face. As I glanced up, I saw Billy. He walked slowly in the distance, alone.

"Billy! Hey, it's Stasia."

He stopped and looked at me, although he didn't seem to recognize who I was.

"Billy!" I said again, before running over to him.

"Oh, Stasia, is that you? I could not hear what you were saying."

"Billy, I was the Lady of Animals and now I am nothing."

He nodded, "You mustn't dwell on the past my dear."

I was hoping for a different response, especially from someone who sought me out to bring me back to Surritz.

"So you know what you did with the diamond right? Where is it? Where did you hide it?" he asked anxiously.

I woke up right before I learned what I had done with

it. It could be anywhere.

Billy rolled his head and looked carefully into my eyes with a direct gaze, as if he was reading my mind. "Do you see how many animals died after you did? They all killed themselves. Yes, Abe did go crazy and they didn't want to be under his rule anymore."

He continued, "Never in history had an animal known the capability of killing oneself."

Billy sat down on the grass—his posture so erect that his paws looked humanlike. "But, their souls are not free. You are not free to inhabit another body and live another life if you commit suicide," he said, shaking his head.

"What happens then?" I asked.

"Well, you simply float around on the same land, invisible to everyone, living out your misery over and over. All the pain the animals felt from Abe is here. It's on a loop, just a replay—over and over about twenty times a day. They can barely sleep. They nod in and out, but then they wake up to the same pain they felt before. This place is what we call the 'in-between'."

Could it be true? The animals were the nicest creatures I had ever known.

"If you want to save them, find and give me the white diamond. With its powers, together we can release all the souls back into their living bodies. Look around you..."

Dark, cold trees lurked for miles into the forest.

"Think of how many of your animal friends' souls are all around you right now. They are trying to touch you, trying to communicate, but they can't. All they feel is their own misery."

He gently ran his paw over my cheek. "Trying to touch you..." he said again, as I imagined them calling to me.

"With the diamond, all the animals can have their bodies back again. They deserve another chance at happiness. Don't you think?" Billy clasped his hands together, his claws intertwined.

"How do I find it? Surritz looks awfully different from when I lived here. Where has the lake gone? Where is the castle Abe and I enjoyed so much? I can't seem to find my way around."

"A lot has changed in fifteen years, that's all."

"How did all the dragons stay?" I asked him.

"The dragons decided that they were not going to kill themselves. Too selfish I guess," he chuckled.

It seemed to be true. I remembered what Elgor had said. The dragons are smart animals, but they can also be very persuaded by selfish thoughts.

"Did you know Abe?" I asked Billy.

"Not personally, but he died shortly after you did."

"So he cannot find me?" I asked.

"Possibly, but he is probably in his next life. Don't worry, he didn't commit suicide. He won't be lurking around you in the 'in-between'." He laughed again. "Actually, he died drowning. He went for a swim in the ocean, and that was it. Never saw him again," he said. "Did you remember how you died in Surritz?" Billy asked. "The murder Abe committed. So tragic what he did to you."

Goose bumps formed on my arms. The thought of seeing Abe scared me. Would he be able to kill me again?

"No. I just can't seem to remember that part," I said.

"That's good. Actually the branch that can take you back in time to that moment is too high. You will never be able to reach it. You don't need to remember all those horrible details anyway." He ran his paws over his feathers, straightening out the stray ones. "You're the only one who knows where the diamond is. I can't believe no one has found it after all these years. Time is fleeting, Stasia," Billy explained.

I thought about how all this would sound to Amelie. She wouldn't be scared. She would know what to do.

I missed her. I wanted to tell her everything about the Tree of Waking Thoughts, the time travel, how I was the Lady of Animals, and how Abe was in St. Michael before we were even born. Who would she think Mayleen was?

Billy stood still, very erect. As daylight broke, light began to peek through the forest. I could smell the dewdrops forming on nearby grass. "I have to get back home. I must find Amelie," I said to Billy.

"Do you know how long you have been in Surritz this time?" he asked.

"Five, six hours?"

He laughed. "Silly girl. Three months, your time. Eleven months our time. You haven't even come out from underneath that tree for any food."

Catching my astonished look, he added, "It's simple—your body was hibernating while your mind was traveling. It's nothing new for animals. And don't worry. I made sure no one bothered you."

The shock must have been apparent on my face. I managed to mutter something about my family being worried.

He didn't seem to care. He didn't react or even move. He just sat there looking at me as if I hadn't expressed concern at all.

Before Billy could even think about speaking again, I started to run through the grass fields, cutting through the trees like a bear.

"Where are you going now?" I heard him say in the distance.

Something grabbed my foot, making me fall, but I didn't bother to check what it was. *Mama must be so worried. What is Pa going to say when he finds out that dragons don't eat at all? Are Maisy and Flynn still in St. Michael? Is Amelie alive?* Reality hit me like a bat to the face. I forgot all about my adventures as Nina; Abe faded from my memory. I didn't care about the diamond. I wanted to go home to my family.

When I neared the ocean, the sea sprayed up at me, hitting me harder than bricks as my heart started to pound.

"LET ME IN!" I screamed. "LET ME IN!"

I needed to go home.

I wanted to go home.

Where was the funnel? How could I find it like this?

I walked along the ocean, running my hand across the seabed. Water collapsed above me, sending me tumbling backwards onto the land. I thought the rock to the funnel was here, but I couldn't find it.

Think Nina…I mean, Stasia! Just think. Breathe. It's here somewhere. Just remember how you got here.

I lay on my belly and slid horizontally into the water. It was easier this way. I inched across the bottom of the sand like a stingray. Finally, when I felt like I couldn't hold my breath any longer, I felt the large rock. I slapped it with my palm and waited for it to send me home.

I ARRIVED back in St. Michael in the afternoon. My three-month journey was confirmed when I reached the island. In the distance, there was no more snow to be seen. Signs of life were evident—palm trees were green, goats were grazing, and even a couple of Sugarbirds flew over my head as I lay on the beach. The sun felt so good on my skin that I was paralyzed. My body sank deeper and deeper into the sand as the ocean waves crashed behind me. It had to be only about sixty-five degrees, but the warmth felt so refreshing. I rolled around— first on my right side, then on my left. Then, I lay flat on my stomach with my head titled forward. I stretched my arms out to feel the soft sand. As I let it run through my hands, I felt the little gems get stuck between my fingers. I didn't need the gems anymore to feel the warmth of the beach, but I had to pick up the aquamarine stone that dazzled in front of me. It was the first time that I saw a blue stone that big.

I looked straight into it and suddenly everything started to shake. The sand trembled. The trees swayed. I could barely recognize the landscape around me as everything started to blur together. I held the gem tightly until I saw a shadow behind me. I saw Amelie!

"Amelie!" I called.

I had found her!

"Amelie! Where have you been? We have all been so desperately looking for you. I'm so glad you are okay!"

Amelie walked right past me as if she didn't hear a word of what I was saying. She stuck her fingers in the water, moved them around, and then shook them as if she was trying to remove something.

Becoming very irritated, I yelled her name again but she continued to fiddle with something in the ocean water. Then she turned around and buried her feet in the sand— kicking it around a little until it looked like she had hit something. I walked closer to where she was standing and knelt down. Her toes stopped moving and she sat down, grabbing a stone out of the sand. It was a black pearl. She held it up to the sunlight and began to smile, before stuffing it in her pocket. Next, she picked up a sapphire and skipped it across the ocean like a rock in a pond. I watched it bounce three times until it went straight down. As it sank, a funnel, twice the size of any I'd encountered, began to open in the sea. I could see the ocean creatures spinning inside it.

"Amelie!"

As she walked closer to the funnel, she didn't respond or even flinch. I reached out to grab her arm, but felt nothing as my hand went right through her. I tried to grab her body again and again, but it was like trying to hold onto thin air. Then she moved and walked into the ocean. She whirled around in the waterspout for several seconds before going straight down. I threw the aquamarine stone down in the sand and ran after her.

"No! Wait."

I was jumping around frantically in the water, but nothing happened. Then, the scene disappeared. The water was calm again. There was no sign of Amelie's footprints in the sand. The premonition was gone.

How did Amelie know about this place? Had she followed me? Why didn't she tell me the truth?

I started walking home from the beach as I turned around idea after idea in my head. Why had Amelie secretly followed me to Surritz?

As I walked into the driveway, I saw her. Amelie. She stood next to the old cast iron gate, her back against the stone wall, leaning right beside the welcome sign. It was no longer covered in snow; we were back to the Forrester family again.

"Amelie!" her eyes remained closed as if she hadn't heard me.

"Amelie?" I repeated.

Slowly, her lips curled on each side of her mouth and

her eyes squeezed shut. The balls of her cheeks turned a reddish color as her perfect smile spread slowly across her face before she spoke.

"Stasia, I've been to Surritz."

CHAPTER 25

AMELIE PULLED the curtains open in one clean sweep. "You're lucky your parents are out. You're going to be grounded for a year when they find out you're still alive!"

As we walked onto the patio, I already had five dubious scenarios rumbling around in my mind. I concluded on the most obvious—Amelie had been involved in this conspiracy from the beginning, knowing exactly why she'd wanted me hypnotized. But did she really think I could contact her mother? Guilt washed over me again for being so selfish.

"There is something I need to tell you…" she trailed off.

"Yes, about Surritz. How did you get there? What did you see," I asked, looking down at the mud we'd tracked in.

"I do feel bad for not telling you before."

"Amelie, I know about your mother," I said.

"Know what? That she died, Stasia?" she answered angrily.

"No, I mean I know you believe me. I know you think I can contact her somehow. You must have been so sad. So angry. Why didn't you tell me?"

Red took over the whites of her eyes.

"I'm sorry for being a bad friend," I said, "I didn't think for one minute to ask you."

When I looked up, Amelie was crying. Tears streamed quickly over her delicate features. Her face sank. She melted into a chair. Her body shook.

"Why did it have to happen?" she asked. "Why? What did I do to deserve this?"

"It's not your fault. But I promise, she's with you."

"How do you know, Stasia? Tell me how you know," she reached out and grabbed my hand.

I held it. "It's ok Amelie."

"Tell me how you know," she said again with her head on my arm.

"I haven't found your mom, Amelie. But with your hypnosis, you know what I did find? That we continue on and on. We never die. We live for eternity."

She stared into my eyes. "I was with her in the hospital when she died," she said, "I've never told anyone this. Not even my father. She did wake up."

I tried to remember the story Mama told me. There was a car crash. Amelie's mother was taken to the hospital in a coma. She stayed for six weeks before Dr. Rose decided to take her off life support. But no one had ever said that she'd woken up.

"What do you mean?" I asked, as she curled up in the chair like a baby.

"Tell me you'll believe me, Stasia. I can't tell you unless you believe me."

The words came out of my mouth before I realized what I was saying. "I believe you."

"She talked to me, like she had never been hurt. Like she was normal. She opened her eyes. She spoke to me."

"Amelie, why didn't you tell your father? Why didn't you say something before?"

"Before she was cut off? You think I killed her by not telling my father?"

"No, no that's not what I mean," I said.

"She told me she wanted to die, Stasia."

Amelie was calmer now, but she still held my hand tightly. She waited for me to react. When I didn't, she continued, "She said that when the other person drove her off the road, she died. But something happened. She wasn't really dead. She saw her body in the car, until she was rushed someplace else. She didn't feel any pain."

"Where did she go?" I asked.

"She told me where she went." Amelie slowly adjusted her eyes so that they met mine again.

"Where did she go, Amelie?" I repeated.

"She told me she went underwater."

I couldn't help but think Amelie did not hear what her mom said. But I wasn't about to question her.

"You said you would believe me," Amelie said.

"I do, but why would she go there?" I asked, "Did she tell you anything else?"

"She said when she died she was free. She could go wherever she wanted. Then she said again that she went underwater. She said when she found the answer she was looking for, she drifted far away from the universe. She said she didn't want to come back."

"So what happened?" I asked.

"She said she was pulled back by the machines. She didn't want me to tell my father that she woke up. She told me that she loved me, but she wanted to die."

More tears came flowing out of Amelie's eyes.

"It's not your fault, Amelie."

"She went to Surritz right? I followed you. When I saw you go there, it all clicked. I just knew that is where she'd gone. I wondered for all these years. What did she need to find out?" Amelie asked.

"Is that why you went there?" I asked her. "Where were you for so long? We all looked for you."

"I went to Mr. Gordon's house and hid out in his guest house. When I saw you go to the beach, I followed you. The only thing that came easily for me was going through the funnel."

If Amelie had gone to Surritz, that means she had lived there before. Had she already known about Abe and the animals, the diamond, and Fabienne?

With all the more important questions in my head, all I said was, "Amelie, that's breaking and entering."

"What's going to happen, Stasia? Mr. Gordon never knew I was there. No big deal."

She wiped away her tears. The emotion in her voice had vanished. On the surface, the carefree girl was back.

"Anyway, I heard the whole conversation you had with your mom and Maisy. I did the same thing you did. I found the gems, picked them up, dove in the water and I was there."

"Why didn't you just ask me?" My face tingled as blood ran through my head.

"I wanted to do it on my own, to see if I could. I was curious about Billy and everything you told me. I never forgot the last words my mother spoke. I needed to go where she went."

"What happened when you got there?" I asked.

"I saw a tree in the distance. It was bigger than the ones in St. Michael. I didn't see anything around me because I felt so compelled to walk towards it. But I turned around, Stasia. I got scared. I didn't know what was happening. I came back to St. Michael.

"Tell me what happens when you go there," Amelie said.

"There's this man, Amelie, and I love him. I was able to travel back in time and be with him. I feel like I know him, like he's here. But he's the one that killed me."

"You're in love with a man that killed you in your past life? And you haven't actually met him in "real time"?" she said sarcastically as she leaned back. Her body began to shake before she let out a loud, long laugh.

"It's not funny…" I said, but thank God she wasn't crying anymore.

I told her everything I found out about Nina and Abe, Mayleen, the monsters, Fabienne, and Billy.

"Well, what are you thinking?" I asked her when she didn't respond.

"Time travel? I think…your emotions are overcoming your reasoning."

Outside, several brown leaves fell from trees, making way for the new life that was emerging. There was hope for summer now.

"Listen, I'm sorry again for telling my dad everything about Billy and Surritz and telling him you were crazy. You're not, well, maybe a little, but I shouldn't have told him anything. I got a new book on past lives, Stasia. We all have them; our memories are just wiped clean when we are born."

"Why is that?" I asked.

"Well, how would you fulfill the contract you make if you remembered all of your experiences?"

What was she talking about?

"Oh, gosh Stasia, you need to start reading. Picking up a book once in a while is not going to kill you."

So we make a contract before we are born. In this contract we dictate what we want from the life we are born into. We decide how we will achieve it, when we will die, and how. Apparently, as a child, I had still thought I was Nina. I had been so confused; I hadn't known what I was doing on Earth. Well, this was all according to Amelie.

"Did you know your soul enters a fetus in the last month before its born? When you're between lives, you pick your fetus…so cool."

"Okay, that's just ridiculous," I replied, "and you think *I'm* the one who has no reasoning?"

"It's true, Stasia."

"You pick your fetus, the angel attorney draws up a contract for your life, and then God signs it?"

"Exactly," she said, giggling.

She collapsed into the chair before turning her head to me. "Stasia, let's go together. Before your parents come home and realize you are still alive. Let's go tonight!"

Her eyes brightened and widened. I could tell by her smile that there was only one acceptable answer. The decision was already made.

* * *

WE JUMPED in the funnel and were transported to the tall, silky grass in Surritz.

"I'm happy just going back and forth. You see that

seahorse? I think he talked to you. Am I dreaming?" Amelie asked.

"Yes, dreaming. Pay attention." I kept walking forward at a steady pace. There was no reason for Amelie to know *everything*. Besides, all he said was, "You again? You come back and forth quite often. You someone special?"

I shifted my eyes downward, pretending not to hear.

Scents from flowers of all shapes and sizes immediately hit my nostrils, as Amelie looked with disbelief upon the foreign land.

"We are here. I cannot believe it. Look, Stasia!" She pointed to a dragon walking on all four legs, "*What* is that?"

"It's Billy! Remember the Ouija board that smelled out Billy? All the tracks in the snow? It was Billy who came to visit me."

Finally, Amelie was silent and all she managed to choke out was, "He is beautiful."

"Billy! Billy! I'm back!" I said, jumping up and down.

Billy kept walking at the same pace until suddenly, he was twenty feet closer.

"And who is this might I ask?" he quietly said, holding out his paw to take Amelie's hand. "You've lived in Surritz before."

"How do you know?" she said.

"Because you've managed to come here. Welcome back. We are very happy to have you here with Nina."

Amelie looked at me, lifted her eyebrows and slowly mouthed the word "Nina?" But I knew she recognized the name from when we did the hypnosis.

"It's Stasia, Billy. Stasia."

"Did you find the stone yet?" He stared at me and my thoughts collapsed under his words.

What would Abe do? Why was I thinking about him? If he was as bad as Billy said, I should have hated him. But I didn't. And I couldn't stop thinking about my life as Nina with him. There was nothing in my past thoughts to suggest that he was anything but honorable.

But something still nagged me. Maybe it was the fact that I didn't know where he was, and he never made himself available to me like Billy did. But, he did when I was a child. How else would Mama have known that I had an imaginary friend named Abe Carlton?

So many questions lingered in my mind. Amelie and Billy floated away from me again, until Billy touched my arm. "Stasia, did you find it or not?"

"She's so spacey sometimes, I'm sorry," I heard Amelie say before I was back in the moment.

"No, I didn't find it. I may never," I said, but it wasn't what I really thought.

"What about all the animals? They must feel, oh, so very... trapped."

I held my breath for a few seconds. I couldn't help but think about what he had said. If I could really help the animals stop their pain, it would be wrong not to do something. Not to try.

"Animals? What's going on?" Amelie's voice seemed far away. "Hello? Stasia?" She shook me and then I blinked and saw her right in front of my face.

Disappointed, Billy sent us on our way where I had to spend the next hour explaining to Amelie what was going on. We played with the colorful beetles, and ran through the fields of dandelions.

"So this is where my mother went," Amelie said, as we lay in the grass. "Why do you think she wanted to come here so badly?"

"Maybe she lived here before, like I did," I said.

"It's the only thing I can think of," Amelie replied. "I miss her, Stasia. I miss her so much."

She didn't speak again until the sun started to go down. We had walked through the woods and stopped by a silver colored pond.

"You've really experienced all this Stasia? I can't believe it. This is crazy."

"See what I mean about no animals being here. Isn't it strange?"

She was too busy watching the flowers on the ground change colors. Each leaf moved separately. They were closing up shop for the night and I saw their petals flutter like butterflies, until they slowly closed.

"What color is this? I have never seen this color in my life." She pointed to a tulip that had long purplish tentacles.

"Did you hear what I said about the animals? Do you think it's true—that they all killed themselves after I died?"

"It's a bit far-fetched. You shouldn't believe everything Billy is telling you."

I shouldn't, but I did. I couldn't help it. There were thousands of animals in my past life and they were all gone now. Something happened.

We dangled our feet in the warm water.

"Look!" Amelie said, pointing to my legs. "The colors—there they go again."

Bright red colors wandered off my toes and into the water. This time, they made zigzags that ran in all directions. I thought about Abe's words to Nina:

It's the knowledge being passed on from one being to another. It's all about awareness.

Ironically, I had the same qualities that Abe had, even in a new life. As I looked out at the water, I finally recognized where I was. The same lake where Abe and Nina used to meet! I had finally found it.

"Strange, the colors in this place. There are no words to describe them. It's like a bright pink, but blue also," Amelie rambled.

"So, how will I know the truth about Abe? I'm not so sure he killed me after all."

"You know he did. Billy told you. Just find the branch on the Tree of Waking Thoughts and find out."

"If he didn't, maybe I will meet him again. I think he is still here. I'm sure of it," I said.

"What about what Billy said? He could be well into his next life—married, happy, and with children. You will never find him then."

"I know, but I have to try."

We both went into the water. It was the perfect temperature—a little cooler than the air, but not cold enough to make us shiver. The whitecaps in the ocean above looked like seagulls diving down from the sky.

Splash! Our heads turned back down as a head popped up beside us.

"Oh, my, well, excuse me. I…was…just swimming. I was doing my daily swimming and wow, I'm so sorry." A large black and white penguin with a long beak and ears rose swiftly out of the shallow water. "Wait, who are you? Where are you from? I have never seen you here before." His expression changed and he eyed the both of us; he was frightened. His beak moved from side to side and his eyes had a nervous tick.

Amelie was finally speechless.

"We are looking for Abe Carlton. Do you know him?" I asked.

"I can't say that I do." The creature looked away, but one of his eyes kept glancing back at us. "But I can't LIE! OKAY!" He began to sob. "I do know him. No one in Surritz can lie!" he screamed, then started to mumble, "Well, except those awful dragons. What gave them the right to be able to? I mean, I know it's a bad thing. Not right. But once in a while, it would be nice. Rather amazing. I could hide. I would never have to say anything—"

"Woah," Amelie interrupted.

And then he stopped. "But I will not tell you. No. No I cannot. You cannot make me. And you never told me who you were." He eyed us suspiciously again.

"I'm Stasia, and this is Amelie. We are from St. Michael."

"I have never heard of such a place and I think you are making it up."

"We can't lie, remember?" I slowly said, having no idea if this was correct.

"That is right! St. Michael. Hmmm. It sounds like such a lovely place." He closed his mouth and smiled. "But, wait. Where is it exactly?" He asked, puzzled.

"Oh, St. Michael is an island in the Caribbean," Amelie said confidently.

"Oh, island, yes. Surritz is an island too," he said looking pleased.

"What is your name?" I asked him.

"My name is Gito," he said happily. "It has been so nice to meet you two. If you would like someone to show you around Surritz, my friend Milo would be happy to do it. Yes, I'm offering her services. I would offer myself, but of course

I cannot leave the water." He frowned.

"Where is Abe Carlton? Does he still live here?" I asked again.

"I know we have become friends, and you have told me about the Care Being. I do trust the both of you. Such nice people you are. But, I would not like to say anything about Abe Carlton at the moment, although I do know who he is. Perhaps after spending some time with my friend Milo, she will tell you about Abe. She can go anywhere and not touch the ground. I'm so jealous. I wish I did not have to touch the ground also." He stared into space, reminiscing about something. "Well, I must be on my way now. I have not even finished half of my swimming. If I do not practice, I will get larger. And I definitely do not wish to get larger."

"How do we find Milo?" Amelie asked.

"Oh. Yes. Milo. Milo can be found at Blootea volcano. It is over there beyond the sierra—all the way in the back. You can't miss it. Largest waterfall in Surritz."

He gave us a hug and dipped his head back into the water. We watched him paddle away quickly before it began to get very dark outside. We could only see the glow of the fish in the water around us.

"It's almost like home, Amelie. Just pretend those fish up there are stars."

She held on to my hand tightly, "I thought you said there were no more animals here."

"He is the first animal besides a dragon that I have seen," I admitted.

Amelie didn't seem to be listening. She was yawning and closing her eyes.

"I'm really tired. Where can we sleep?" she asked.

CHAPTER 26

AFTER A good night's sleep in Fabienne's guesthouse, we headed to Blootea volcano early in the morning, before Fabienne woke up, before she knew we were even there.

"Must be a bird," Amelie said to me confidently, about Milo. "Gito said she's an animal that can go everywhere, but doesn't touch the ground or the water."

She was more energetic today, feeling the ground, smelling the grass, touching everything as if she felt some sort of vibration. I wondered how much of this she had picked up reading in the past life, voodoo, hypnosis, or whatever-you-call-them books.

It felt like we had been walking for hours on end. The scenery kept changing, but everything felt the same. We saw the same birds, the same river, the same cottages, and the same trees.

"Are we walking in a circle?" Amelie interrupted, as I was thinking the same thing.

"We've been walking forever, but the sun is still in the same spot, nothing seems to be changing," I said.

But then I caught Amelie staring at something in the

distance. When I looked over, I saw it too. It was a large chestnut oak tree, swaying heavily in a non-existent breeze.

"That gold color, it's so beautiful," said Amelie. "I saw this tree the last time I came to Surritz."

When all I saw was a green tree, I knew what we had stumbled upon. It was Amelie's Tree of Waking Thoughts. When she stepped in the direction of the tree, attracted to it like a magnet, it started moving backwards so quickly that eventually it vanished.

"I'm not scared of it anymore. I wanted to check it out, but now I can't see it anymore," Amelie said.

"It's not the right time. When you need it, it will be there, trust me."

We took a break to sit down in the grass. The sun was beaming and we couldn't stop sweating. The grass was tall, surrounding us on all sides. Just as I was getting comfortable on my back, soaking in the sunlight that burned on my face, I heard Amelie shuffle through the bushes.

"What on earth is that? Is it a home?" Amelie asked.

I caught up with her to see what looked like a grass igloo.

It was tiny—no bigger than a small bucket. The entrance was a hole far smaller than my body could fit. We both got down on our hands and knees to peer inside. The grass was wet and cold.

"Hello? Is anyone there?" I called through the hole.

My voice echoed back at us three times louder.

"From the sound of it, it must be a pretty big home," I told Amelie.

I started to smell the sweet scent of freshly baked cranberry bread. I could see the scent travel out through the hole, conforming itself into the shape of a dragon, and dancing around my face.

"Hello! Anyone home?" Amelie cried out, trying to squeeze through the hole.

A patch of grass surrounded the igloo shaped home and had white and yellow lilies growing as tall as half the house.

"Hello? Who's there?" an answer came back. "Is that you, Stasia?"

My blood raced through my veins. *Abe?*

"Yes, it's me. Who's in there?" I said, backing away.

And then a laughing melody came floating to us. Thick, green feathers were pushing their way out of the hole. The poor thing looked stuck.

"Do you need some help, sir?" I asked.

"Pull it out," said Amelie, impatiently.

When I turned back to the entrance, Billy's head greeted me. I sighed.

"How did you find me? What are you doing here?" he said.

"Billy, do you live in there?" I asked.

"Yes, welcome to my second home when I'm not in the ocean. I'd invite you in but you'd never fit. The hard part is getting through the door. My house is quite big, otherwise. Runs underground for about half a mile that way." He pointed towards the volcano. "The roots from these flowers go into my living room. We hang lamps, pots, all sorts of things from them."

"So that explains it. Do all the animals live underground? No wonder we never see any," I said to him.

After I said it, I remembered what Gito told me about the dragons being able to lie. If it were true, was Billy lying about all the animals killing themselves in my previous life?

Just play it cool, Stasia.

I was becoming a much better detective than I previously thought possible.

"I already explained to you where all the animals have gone, Stasia," Billy said, his red tail becoming erect and still. His voice lowered and his eyes squinted. I tried not to look at Amelie, because I knew she was staring at me, dying to comment.

Too late.

"How do you explain Gito then?" she interrupted on her own. "He seems pretty animalish to me."

Billy moved his ears several times before holding his composure and gently grinning back at us. "Well, how did you two meet Gito? I see you've been exploring."

All the garden flowers squealed in unison and tried to inconspicuously shut their petals, as if it were nighttime.

"Gito is a water creature. He cannot walk on land. Like I said, all *land* animals are gone. Have you seen any animals walking around? Besides my breed of course."

He paused purposely.

"Didn't think so," he answered his own question.

I had so many more questions about the land animals, but I didn't feel comfortable asking them with Amelie around.

"So, where exactly are you guys heading?" he asked slowly.

"To find the diamond for you." I squeezed Amelie's hand, praying she knew what this signal meant. "I'm going to look at the volcano," I said to Billy.

Billy eyed me suspiciously. He walked around the both of us, putting his claws on my shoulder, and smelling something in my hair. He seemed to buy my story for the time being. I guess we were capable of lying after all.

"You are going the wrong way," he said after a couple minutes. "It's back that way." He turned around and pointed. "When you get there, you'll know."

"I'm sure we will find it," Amelie said, fidgeting with her clothing. She turned to me and gently nodded towards the volcano with her head.

She was ready to go.

"Just bring it back here then, okay? I will take care of everything after that."

"Ready, Amelie?" She was more willing and ready then I ever wanted to be.

Billy shook our hands excitedly, before poufs of feathers flew into the air as he stuffed his body back inside the front door. He closed it with what seemed to be driftwood attached to a couple nails. There were small letters written in the middle.

DO NOT ENTER. PRIVATE RESIDENCE.

"Weird house, don't you think?" Amelie asked as we left. "Definitely not my style."

"Because you'd mess up your hair going in and out?"

"Exactly."

Finally, the sun changed its position. It seemed to be setting and the landscape, as a result, was changing. The tall grass was behind us. We were walking towards big, tropical trees. The air was thicker, wetter. We were getting closer to our destination.

When we stood only yards from Blootea volcano, we both gazed up in awe. The ocean masked the peak, as it crashed back into itself.

"That's where the jewels are made," I said to Amelie.

"St. Michael gems?"

"Before they fall, they are in their purest form. Forms that can heal anybody and grant anyone the power to fulfill their dreams."

"Like what?" she asked.

"I don't know. Anything," I answered.

She pulled out the black pearl from her pocket. "You think this one has powers?"

It was bigger and shinier than I had seen in my premonition of her on the beach.

"I don't know. Try something."

"How?"

"Ask a question."

"You're supposed to be the expert," Amelie said.

"Just ask something already."

She held the pearl above her head. "Magic pearl of the Surritz land, please make me taller like Stasia."

"What? You want to be taller?"

"Of course, Stasia. Who doesn't? Along with a long list of other things: lighter hair, smaller eyebrows, and prettier hands. You should be thankful for those hands. I have always envied them."

Amelie envies my hands *and* she cries. I couldn't believe it.

"Ok, enough about me. You have to ask something that contributes to humanity, not vanity!" I said.

She then said something I wasn't expecting. "Okay, black magic pearl of the land of Surritz, show me where my mother is."

A beautiful hum surrounded us like bees flying in a group. The sound traveled around our bodies several times before my vision started to blur. The images went around and around my face very quickly, until they started to rearrange themselves.

What I thought were bees were in fact letters! The letters buzzed in front of me and frantically arranged themselves to form words.

As they floated around, I could finally read what was written: SIT DOWN AND WRITE AMELIE.

Whoever this was, they must have known we got the message, because a second later, the letters started bouncing and buzzing again. They made three quick laps around me before the vision disappeared completely. I closed my eyes, blinking them rapidly. Amelie stared ahead. Was she in shock? Why wasn't she elated?

"See, worthless," she said.

"Amelie, you didn't see it?"

She looked at me carefully. "You think this is funny?"

"No, I saw words. 'Sit down and write Amelie.' Right in front of my face."

Hope returned to her. "Was it her?"

"I don't know. But whoever it was, they definitely addressed you."

"Why couldn't I see it then? And what did it mean? What am I supposed to write?"

"Maybe your mom wants you to write her a letter," I said, guessing.

Amelie cusped the pearl tightly and carefully wrapped it in a pink handkerchief before she put it back in her pocket. "We have to find out."

Given her spontaneous personality, I thought she'd want to go back to Fabienne's house to start writing, but instead, she said, "When we get back to St. Michael. Let's get this done first. I don't want to get stuck here... with the dragons."

"Me neither," I said, as we made our way to the volcano.

"Wow, it's big," Amelie gasped. "I've never seen a volcano before. Can we go inside?"

"Are you crazy, that waterfall will kill you."

"Or will it give you powers?" Amelie raised her eyebrows up and down. "There are also fish that talk to you in a funnel, and animals that kill themselves, and dragons want diamonds…in a land that exists below the ocean!"

A crazed laughter forced through my mouth. My belly expanded so many times that my sides ached. I hadn't laughed this hard in a long time. "Can't disagree with you there."

A pack of dragons found their way to us shortly after we settled by the bottom of the volcano.

"Hello, there," one of the bigger ones said, as four more surrounded us.

"What ya'll looking for? We can help you," said the baby.

"The gem," Amelie blurted out.

All the dragons stood up on their hind legs and their faces dropped. Their little whiskers twitched.

"What's that?" one said.

"Oh, no, never heard of that. What is it? Is it a stone or, ummm, grass or something?" the baby said again.

"It's nothing," I interrupted.

"Do you guys know Billy by any chance?" Amelie asked, making me cringe.

"Yes. Yes, we do actually. You have business with him?" the large male said.

"He's a friend," I answered.

They all relaxed back down on all four legs. The two

smallest ones let out sighs of relief.

"Well, why didn't you say so before?" the mother asked.

"We love Billy," said the baby. "He's our uncle."

"Oh, cool! Billy is great, isn't he?" I said through my teeth, grinning at Amelie.

"Yes, we see Billy every day. He never mentioned us? I'm Amelie, and this is Stasia."

"It's very nice to meet you two. Now, what can we help you with? Are you new to Surritz?"

"Yes, sort of. We are looking for some stones," I said.

"Which ones? There aren't many left. Wish we could get our hands on the diamond," the mother said looking at the other three and laughing.

"That would be redemption day." She laughed again, causing the little ones to giggle too.

Amelie and I joined.

"Well, where *is* that diamond?" I asked still laughing.

"We think it's on the top of Blootea, by the peak," one of the young ones said. "But we are trying to find out. Right mommy?"

"Yes, sweetie. That's right. Uncle Billy tell you that?"

The little one smiled as if she knew a big secret. "He's working on finding it."

"You can't find out? I'm sure you all could climb or fly to those boulders in no time," Amelie said.

All of their expressions changed.

"We could," said the father, "but obviously we don't."

"Why?" I said, still amused.

"The Master of Animals assigned vicious creatures to reign over Blootea Peak, unfortunately."

"Oh yeah, Abe? How?" I asked. "Isn't the Master of Animals supposed to love animals?"

They all paused and looked at us suspiciously.

"We better be on our way," the father said. "Let's go kids."

He motioned for all of them to turn around. He was already nudging them. They scampered away quickly, running into bushes as they turned around to make sure we weren't following them.

"You blew it," Amelie said, "You're asking too many questions. Just let me do the talking next time. Now, what's the next step?"

A cooing noise rumbled through the sound of the waterfalls.

"Look!" Amelie pointed above.

An eagle was flying towards us. Large teeth hung out from its lips. Teeth? Yes, pointy like wolves.

"INNNCOMMING," the animal squawked.

As it got closer, it made two circles around us, blinking its big eyes quickly, making more incoherent noises.

"I'm Milo!" Her wings flapped as fast as a hummingbird. "Jump aboard." She unrolled her wing like a long carpet. "I'm sure I can take both of you."

Without any reluctance, we both climbed up her ribbed, feathered wing.

"Gito told me to look for you two," she said, "I can smell you from a mile away!"

"Where are we going?" asked Amelie.

"We are going up, up and away. Be prepared!" she soared.

While I was shaking, Amelie looked excited.

"So there's only one reason you guys must be here.

Looking for some stones are you?"

"Yes," we both said simultaneously.

"I know where they are, don't worry," Milo replied.

Over the next hour, we soared through the waterfall. The water beat so hard on our heads that I thought they would explode. Even brave Amelie was scared and admitted that she wanted to go back home. But, I knew we were doing the right thing because through the strands of water, I saw colors and shapes again.

"Look!" Milo swooped down so quickly my hair stood straight up and the wind choked me. "Catch it. It's falling, look!"

A bright, green emerald was falling from the top of the volcano. Milo navigated through the water just in time for the two of us to reach out our hands.

"To the left!" I screamed, "Faster, go down. To the right. Quickly Milo!"

The emerald glowed even underneath the falling water! It touched the tips of my fingers but I missed it and it kept falling.

"Straight down Milo. Faster!"

She flew down until we were side by side with the emerald. It was big—about the size of a dime.

"Amelie, put out your hands!" I yelled, and the both of us clasped our hands in the air until I wrapped my palm around the stone.

"Got it!"

"Woohoooo!" yelled Milo, as she whisked back around in the air and soared higher towards the top of the volcano.

"Do these stones have the same powers as the ones on St. Michael?" Amelie's face lit up.

"I don't know. I haven't really encountered too many of them in Surritz," I replied.

"Only a few people can release the power of these stones," Milo said, as she flew faster and higher. "Are you one of them?"

Amelie and I looked at each other in surprise.

"How do we find out?" I asked Milo.

"Hold it in your fist and wait. If nothing happens in two minutes, it's useless. It's just another pretty stone."

I gripped the gem tightly, hoping something would happen.

CHAPTER 27

ONE MINUTE later, something occurred. A voice spoke to me and I recognized it immediately. There was no one that had a voice like his. Abe spoke softly, but clearly. The surrounding water noise was blocked out as I focused on his words: "When you encounter someone, look at them and say this secret motto to see how everything will turn out: 'Gone with the stones are the one.' If you see their heads turn to skulls and black crows fly away, they have broken the peace. If everyone smiles and comes closer, they have lived up to their promises. This is the word of Dr. Sally."

And in a flash, his voice was gone and I was aware of where I was again.

"Abe, where are you?" I asked into the cold, wet air.

"What did you say?" said Milo. "You've heard of Abe?"

"I am Nina. I am the Lady of Animals." I told her.

Milo stopped flying upward and flapped her wings in place while she turned her head completely around to face us.

Amelie was frightened, again.

"How do you know about Nina and Abe?" Milo eyed

us both suspiciously.

"No one can lie here, remember? I need to find my diamond."

"It's awful what happened. All the land animals have gone." Milo said. "My family used to live on land. We all died. I haven't communicated with them since... since I came back."

"What do you mean? What happened?" Amelie asked.

"I don't know. One day, I came back in this body. But it's not mine. It's horrifying! The same thing happened to Gito. He used to be a beautiful horse. "

"Let's just keep going." I said, before Milo began to tear up. "I'm sure we will find an explanation."

I looked up into the fog and rain. Sand and leaves blew fiercely through the wind. It wasn't going to be an easy feat.

"The peak of Blootea is in the ocean. It goes up about five feet. That's where your diamond is. I have never told anyone that. But, guarding the diamond are sea creatures you have never seen before and could never imagine. They are called the Soulless Swimmers. They are dangerous, but if you are as you say, they cannot harm you. Don't be afraid," said Milo.

"How will I get the stone?" I asked her.

"Just swim right past them. The diamond sits in the middle of the red coral. Your friend will have to stay here or else she will get hurt."

Amelie was relieved. "Yes, I'll just wait here, Stasia. You go ahead."

"I'll fly up to the water and you must jump. Swim upwards with all your might, but don't fall. Before you come back, stick your head out and make sure you jump on to my back. It's a long way down if you miss…"

Was that an attempt at a joke? Amelie's face was white and this time she said nothing.

"I'm ready," I said.

Milo soared close to the water. The waves crashed upwards and fell as salty rain. Her wings got tangled in the ocean water and she rocked back and forth like a sailboat in a storm.

"Wwwhhhooaaa, whoa!" She yelled as her eyes instantly doubled in size.

"Jump, Stasia! Jump!" I heard both of them yelling at me. I stood up on Milo and dug my hands into the icy water. I propelled my arms up and down until I could feel myself lifting away from Milo. And then, the ocean water sucked me right in as if I belonged there.

It was not murky like I expected. It was stormy outside, but it was calm underneath the water. I passed several seahorses, puffer fish, and needlefish that warned me.

Don't go.
Turn back.
It's the end here.
There's nothing here for you.
Watch out.
Right in front of you.

The warnings didn't stop, but only increased in intensity as I got closer and closer to the coral. I didn't worry about holding my breath because for some reason, I was able to swim so fast in the water that it seemed as if only a couple seconds had passed.

As I swam past the frightened fish, I saw Pa's face in

the mask again. He was poking me, motioning, trying so hard for me to see the needlefish. I did, he smiled and the water filled his mask and snorkel. But then, instead of going back up to the ocean's surface like we had, I pictured my fantasy ending. He took the mask off, grabbed my hand, and we raced through the ocean like two tunas in a pack. We followed the needlefish for hours as they swam through the waters. We even became invisible and Pa and I were able to touch them. He put his hand on my face and we hugged. He was proud. I was happy.

That vision quickly faded as I felt a wave of cold water wash over my back. I looked around quickly, but nothing was there. The needlefish were gone. There was nothing in the water. Just when I thought I was never going to find the red coral, I saw something in the shadows in front of me.

Floating like a bubble in the air was a beautiful, bright, large zigzagged piece of red coral. And its protectors came out of nowhere, standing like militia ready to fire. The Soulless Swimmers were nothing short of horrifying. The awful creatures had no heads but instead, ten human arms and tough scales.

I held my eyes tightly shut and began to repeat the motto in my head, *Gone with the stones are the one. Gone with the stones are the one. Gone with the stones are the one.*

Suddenly, I saw the heads they used to have. Human heads! And then they transformed as their skin flew off behind them and their heads turned to skulls. Black crows flew out from all directions and their heads fell downward. I felt sorry for these fallen ones, as clearly they had done something that could never be redeemed. I closed my eyes again and swam as fast as I could into their circle, and towards the red coral.

As I neared it, I remembered the glowing leaf I had taken from the Tree of Waking Thoughts. I reached into my pocket and held on to it tightly, hoping somehow it would give me courage. Immediately, I felt that I was protected and then, as if I had never left that moment in time, I experienced the way I had died.

CHAPTER 28

I RECOGNIZE this man's voice. "Attention, attention! We are about to begin!" he says. He is the tall man who helped put Elgor back in the water when Abe returned from Earth.

He screams to the crowd in the castle's garden. People are lined up in all directions, ready for the annual Surritz match of hide and seek. But this year, the game involves the animals as well. Abe and I have successfully communicated the thoughts and desires of animals to humans. Humans are ready to listen to the feelings of animals. I feel so accomplished when I see that people understand our roles as Master and Lady of Animals. They can finally see the energy that is created and flowing through all of us.

"And now the rules!" he shouts into the crowd. "My name is Fredard Rover and I am the judge of this game. We are going to reach into this basket and each person from Team One will pick his opponent. Team One is Team Abe, Team Two is Team Nina."

Team Abe has all the animals, while my team consists of all the humans. It is only fair to split the two masters up, to make the game more interesting.

"Now, humans, don't feel as though you need to go easy on the animals. Just because every one of them is the oldest of their kind, doesn't mean they are not still quick and smart!" Fredard jokes.

The castle looks small from the outside, but the garden is ten miles wide and spotted with smaller castles throughout the grounds. All of the little castles are in limits for the game.

Fredard jumps up and down as everyone claps. It is a beautiful day for the game. A cool salty breeze breaks up the sun's midday heat.

"One hundred and six players means half the winners. The winners will then play each other and the game will continue for the next couple weeks until we have our grand slam Surritz Superhero! And now…the prizes!"

"What will I do with my winnings?" I joke to Abe, while Fredard reads the list.

"We have Juni on our team. Not only is she more than five times your age, but she can also fly! We *definitely* have the advantage," he replies.

"You may have the oldest animals, but we have chosen the smartest people. They will take down all your animals," Fabienne says.

We laugh.

"And now, for the winner of them all, the prize is… drumroll please. A…trip….redeemable…for…life…to…" He pauses briefly. "Are you ready folks? Are you all ready?" Fredard says.

Everyone screams and stomps one foot, or hoof, or paw, on the ground, waving in the air and chanting, "Tell us, tell us."

"A trip to EARTH!" screams Fredard. "Let's all thank Toro for that one!"

More cries go through the crowd. People hug each other. Women cry. Children holler.

Abe is definitely not happy about the prize that Toro donated. Since Abe's estrangement to him, he has started to give lectures about the way of life on Earth. These included speeches about the ability to fly through the air at over 500mph in a "plane", and speed through the ocean at over 100mph on a "boat". He told of devices that can transport you through a screen called a "computer", and supply music that can be heard anywhere, anytime, and all the time, courtesy of a "radio"!

To Surritzies, Earth is like a fairy tale. And Toro does know where the funnel is. After all, he is the one who told Abe how to find it.

After everyone quiets down, it is time to choose opponents. Fredard throws the slips of paper with everyone's name up in the air. They float upwards with the salty breeze, until the glow fish are able to stick their tails out and grab them. The glow fish are so excited about their crucial role in this annual game. They swim around each other, fighting to grab a winning ticket. If their person or animal wins the whole game, their prize is a trip out of the ocean and into the pond in the middle of the grand entryway of the castle, for a whole year. Here, they will be fed all the best food, daily. Beautiful corals and gems of their choice will surround them. They'll even be given a mate, if that's what they want.

"Fabienne, your opponent will be…" Fredard pauses, while pointing to glow fish number one. Glow fish number one sticks his head out of the water and releases the piece of paper, which falls down directly into Fredard's hand. "It will be…Gito!"

Gito trots out of the middle of the crowd and bows his head to Fabienne. She grabs his mane, and he swings herself on top of his back.

Fredard goes down the list of the humans, pairing them with Sparky, Jack, and Imma.

"And now, Abe!" says Fredard, and all the animals bow to him. "You my friend are paired with…" He waits for the piece paper to touch his hand. "You are paired with Milo!"

Milo walks out of the crowd, with her beautiful shining red and brown coat.

"Who better to be paired with than a beautiful fox?" Abe tells Milo, and she brushes against him before licking his hand.

"And last, but not least," says Fredard to me after everyone else has their opponents. "There should be only two of you left. Come out of your hiding spots, whoever you are…"

Everyone looks around quietly, until there is some noise in the far corner.

"Who is it? Who is it?" asks Fredard.

I look around anxiously. Abe smiles, happy with the selections.

"Oh, here we are," says Fredard. "It is…Nina versus Toro! Okay now. Team Nina will be the hiders, and Team Abe will be the seekers."

THE GAME starts at 9:00 in the morning, as the players go into the gardens. If the hider cannot be found by 2:00 PM, he will win. If he is found, the seeker will be the winner.

There are many places to hide in the castle's grounds. The gardens are like a maze, with big tropical trees and plants in one area, and open fields in the next. Dotted randomly throughout are the smaller castles. Some consist of just a bathroom, while others have eight rooms, lavishly decorated with marble floors, emerald roofs, and sea wood furniture. The only rule to the game is that nothing can be broken or the consequences will be immediate disqualification.

I walk through the gardens that I know so well, stopping only to check my surroundings for places to hide. Just as I suspect, people and animals from both teams are hiding under rocks and in big banana leaves as teammates from team Abe make their way through the forest, peering through the water and checking hidden places under tree branches and in bushes.

I decide to make my way to the castle in the back of the forest. This castle is the most beautiful, and the quietest place on the grounds. Inside, it looks like all the castles— lined with candles, spotless floors, old wooden tables, and large empty rooms.

But, below the exterior is a cemetery. All the fallen people and animals are buried in the basement.

As I make my way down the steps, I recognize the musty smell of the room I visited not long ago, when Dr. Sally was buried. Looking around, I see all the familiar names of the ones that died. The newly buried have shiny copper plaques next to their cemented burials. Saddened, I make my way around the basement, remembering that Dr. Sally told Abe to tell me something.

"The motto will help her in her quest to find purity," I overheard Dr. Sally say.

Abe always said he would tell me when the time was

right. I am determined to ask him today. Right after the game.

As I make my way around the cold, musty basement, I forget all about the game. Memories flood my mind as I think about all the fun times I had with each person and animal that is now gone. I close my eyes and brush my fingers along each tomb.

Then, I hear footsteps.

The game! I think. I run through the small corridors, opening doors and shutting others. It gets darker and darker as I make my way further down more and more steps. The smell changes from a musty scent to an earth like one, the smell of dirt. I am now running through tunnels that are barely lit. I have never been this far below before.

I continue to hear the person following me. Exhausted from all the running, I throw one of the candles in the nook in the wall to the floor. It burns out and it's dark where I stand. Jumping up, I stuff my feet around myself as I climb in the nook, hoping the person will run past me.

It doesn't feel like a game anymore, and surely this part of the basement is off-limits. I struggle to change positions. In the distance there is no one to be seen. The sounds are gone.

I stay still for a few moments, before I see a shadow. Someone is jumping from side to side. As he gets closer, passing a candle on the wall, I see that it's Abe! Did he follow me? And then I hear someone else.

"I've found you," a voice calls out from behind him.

I feel his intentions. I duck in between another nook in the wall, as Abe runs past me, closely followed by Toro. Quietly, I quickly follow them both.

At the end of the tunnel, there are more steps, spirals. Abe and Toro go down, gripping the edge, throwing themselves past several steps at once until they hit ground. But this ground is just dirt. There is nowhere else to go.

"I have to Abe," says Toro. "It's time."

He stands at the bottom, motionless. I want to jump down the steps, but I am frozen. I can't move. My mind is screaming, but I can't speak.

"We don't need a master," says Toro, before pulling out a torch and lighting it with his fiery breath. He swings quickly, nailing Abe in the head. Blood starts to run down his forehead. Toro stands still for a moment, watching Abe fall, before he begins running back the other way, up the steps. But something makes him stop, and he turns around at the top of the stairs. "I'm sorry Abe. I'm sorry."

I duck back into the nook as he runs past me, heading back up the tunnels.

I am unable to react until I hear Abe moaning below.

"Abe!" I scream and jump down. He is lying on his side, blood running down his head.

"It's okay Nina, we all die," he says faintly. "I told you, I was scared this was going to happen."

"Hang in there. I'll get help! I'll go now!" I say.

He moans again and tells me to stay.

"I'm close," he says. "I'm almost gone".

"No!" I scream. "No, please!"

"Nina, listen to me." He says in a whisper. "I love you. I really do."

I cry, but I'm unable to say anything. My mouth is frozen.

"I'm going to St. Michael now. Meet me there, Nina, meet me there."

Before I can ask him what he means, he is gone. He is motionless on the ground. I shake, scream, and cry, before I bang my head against the dirt, but nothing wakes him.

CHAPTER 29

I EMERGE from the castle grounds covered in blood and dirt. I scream for help but I don't see anyone in the vicinity. Then I remember the game. Everyone is hiding.

Meet me there Nina.

His words and sweet breath stay with me in my mind. I run to the place where Abe left for Earth three years ago. Leaves are sticking to the blood on my clothes and I am frantic. I'm tripping over rocks and broken branches. When I reach the edge of the water, I throw myself in and start jumping up and down.

"Take me there, please, just take me there," I cry.

I watch as the blood runs down the sides of my legs. His blood.

The salt water goes into my eyes. "Take me up!"

But nothing happens. Nothing happens for a long while.

When I am half unconscious with grief, Elgor sticks his head out of the water.

"I heard your cries through the ocean," he says, "What's wrong?"

"Meet me there, he said, meet me there," I say, exhausted. My eyes are swollen and I can barely see. My vision blurs and Elgor's nose looks distorted.

Before he can ask I say, "Abe. Arlo. He said meet me there."

Somehow I manage to blurt out the story and the dragon says the one thing I don't want to hear.

"He's dead, Nina. The only way he's going to St. Michael is in another life. He's got many lives ahead of him."

He thinks he's being consoling, but it just makes me weep more.

"He wants me to meet him in St. Michael. I have to go there!" I cry.

I finally hear the story about Arlo.

Even though Abe could stay on Earth for a while, he couldn't live there forever. His life was on Surritz, and he was drawn back to it. I could never go to St. Michael and live as if I was born there, Elgor explains.

"The only way to meet him in St. Michael is to be born in that lifetime," he says as if it's obvious.

"So he wants me to meet him there in another life? I just don't understand," I say.

"You choose where you want to incarnate next," says Elgor. "Where there's a will there's a way."

As he continues the story about Arlo and Mayleen, of how they met, and what happened, I only remember one thing.

"How long is three years in Earth time?" I ask.

He is perplexed for a minute.

"There's a difference in time. Tell me. What is it?" I ask again impatiently.

He calculates something in his mind, going over the

figures a few times. He then comes up with a number and says, "nine months."

The next thing I know I am running back into the woods. I no longer have blood on me but I am covered in a mix of sand and sticky salt water that has hardened on my body like concrete. I am sure Toro went back to Abe's body to search for the diamond. He was always jealous of it. But he doesn't know that Abe gave it to me and that together we hid it far away into the ocean, where no one can ever retrieve it.

As I am running through the small corridors, the light gets dimmer and dimmer. There is a different smell down below. The smell of death. When I reach Abe's body again, his mouth is wide open in a stiff manner. His skin has begun to sink around his face, revealing a large pointy nose and hollow eye sockets.

The little dragon is exactly where I thought. Right by his side.

"I have the diamond," I call to him from the top of the steps. "I have it right here in my pocket. If you want it, you will have to kill me too."

There is remorse in Toro's face and he is stunned to see me.

"How did you find me?" he asks.

"I was here the whole time. The diamond is in *my* pocket."

He is hesitant but he approaches, panicking. I can tell that he is starting to go dizzy. The emotions are getting to him. When he tries to throw me down the steps, I let him.

"It's in my pocket," I say again, as I lie down on the ground. He goes for my pocket and I grip my hands around nothing inside. He struggles with my hands before he uses the same torch to stab me in the right side of my neck. I let him.

Don't be scared. It's almost done.

And then I feel the pain. I shut my eyes and the first day I met Abe flashes into my mind. It's sunny and beautiful. He's in the castle. His surprise at seeing me there makes me smile. Then he is laughing, smiling with his perfect mouth. He's holding my hand. He's hugging me.

I can feel the animals. Their soft fur and smiling faces. Their innocent intentions. Their love. I picture Bisket who I loved more than anything. I hope that I will see Bisket again someday.

I think of Fabienne. Where is she now? Probably hiding where she always does, thinking nobody knows about the treehouse we built. Everyone knows about that place.

Then I see Abe again. This time we are both in the garden in the castle. He's eating the herbs and tickling me. We chase each other around. The animals are laughing and our two children are with us. The children I always hoped would come someday. The sun feels so good on my skin and I close my eyes and lean my face towards it.

And then, I am back on the floor of the castle. I hold my hand to my neck; the blood pounds against my fingers, fighting to break out of my body. I'm slumped down to my knees. I look for Toro again, but he's gone.

Let me go... I think. *I want to be Mayleen's baby*, I command quietly to whoever is listening, hoping the baby had not yet been born.

Then I hear water. A beautiful trickling of water. Waves. As I look behind me, I notice the little door that opens. Water does not flood the tunnel but a bright blue sea light enters. I stick my hand into the sea and it pulls me in until my whole body is immersed. I am swimming upwards. My red blood floats away in the clear water behind me. I feel myself slowing down until I know that I am not swimming any longer, but floating away with the current. I am going upwards, passing Surritz. As I look through the ocean to the land, I see Toro immerging from the castle into the woods. He falls to the ground cursing himself as tears pour down his face. He sobs. Screams. Cries. But I don't have any emotions anymore. I am on a journey.

I keep floating upwards until I pass the top of the land. My view is now all ocean. Miles and miles of calm water. There is no noise underwater and a peaceful feeling sweeps over me. I am running out of breath and can feel the salty water as it starts to leak into my lungs. The pain from my neck is gone but the bloody trail can still be seen in my wake. The water fills my whole body slowly as if I am a fish that belongs to the sea.

My last thought is about Abe.

Meet me there Nina.

I will, I think as I remember the winner's prize for the hide and seek game.

I've already won it.

CHAPTER 30

FROM ONE second to the next, I had gone from dying to being very much alive. *Was it true? Abe was my real father?* I had no time to think about my life as Nina. I was back in the ocean, but this time the Soulless Swimmers were right in front of my eyes. Their many hands grabbed and tore at me, but I swam steadily without fear, for I knew that if I let fear into my mind, I would never recover the diamond. The red coral was big, but I knew where the stone rested. When I was close to it, the creatures formed a circle around me and all I could see were fingers with long red nails grabbing and swinging at me from all directions.

But right in the middle of the coral I saw the thing that I had been looking for. The white diamond reflected my appearance in its perfect translucent glare. Staring back at me was Nina. She was smiling and her hair was moving in the wind again. I knew in that moment that she was not gone. That she and I were the same.

When I picked up the diamond, I was suddenly in the forest where I met Bisket for the first time. It seemed like years since I had been in that very spot, but Bisket was so real in this moment. I knew instantly that she was not gone either.

I held the diamond tightly in my fist as Milo had told me to do with the emerald. Looking downward, I saw the human arms swinging in all directions. Roars and moaning sounds rumbled through the water. I kicked my feet, closed my eyes and traveled downward until I gasped for air and felt the fog brush by my face.

"Stasia!" Amelie's voice echoed. "Over here!"

"I can't see!" My eyes stung as I fought to see clearly through the salty water.

I extended my free hand until I felt Milo's soft feathers.

"It's okay. Jump! Now!" Amelie screamed.
It took everything I had to stop paddling and let myself fall. It was only a couple feet, but I felt like I was falling for a lifetime.

* * *

WE STARED at the volcano and the water that still howled, though now in the distance.

"What are you going to do with the diamond?" Milo asked now that we were safely back on the ground. In my head, I could still hear the sounds of the creatures.

"I will make things right for you. For all the animals."

"It's not possible. They are all gone. I have no idea where they went. I don't know how I came back, and why I was put in this mangled body."

"I think I know," I replied. "You're much prettier as a fox anyway."

She smiled and we said goodbye to Milo. As the sun was setting, we began our journey back to Fabienne's house.

Amelie held my hand silently for some time. It felt good to have her with me, to confirm that I wasn't crazy.

"So, did you see Abe up there?" Amelie asked.

"No, but I found out it was Toro who killed the both of us."

"Who?"

"Just another dragon I once knew."

"*Figures*," she stressed as we walked quietly through the meadows. "So Billy was lying to you about Abe killing you?"

"Seems so," I said.

It was warm and the humidity felt good on my face. For the first time in weeks, I missed home. I even missed the boring life I thought I hated. I wondered how Billy had found me in St. Michael. How was he able to transcend lands? Baldamere's prophecies were right.

I lay awake that night listening to the wind travel through Fabienne's chimney. Amelie was fast asleep but I wondered what our fate was. Were we playing with fire—testing our destiny by traveling back to a previous land and recovering memories of past lives? Would there be consequences? Was my family still looking for me?

I pictured them searching the whole island like a pack of wolves, asking every neighbor and stranger if they'd seen me, the same way we'd done for Amelie. I had been gone for months. Did Maisy and Flynn go back to Puncchit? What did they think happened to me? I unclenched my hand and studied the diamond. It was the first time today that I was alone to view it.

Please, tell me more, I thought. *Tell me what to do next.*

BANG BANG!

A knock on the door interrupted my thoughts.

"Who's there?" I called.

No answer.

BANG BANG!

I dragged myself out of the wooden bed and opened the door slowly. My worst thought would be to see Toro standing in the doorway. Was he still alive?

Instead, it was Fabienne. She motioned for me to come into the hallway and not to wake Amelie. "You're here. I knew it."

"You're my sister," I said before she could say anything more. "I remember so much about you. So many good memories. Aunt Agnes and Uncle Pete, what happened to them? Why didn't you tell me?"

"Toro confessed to us what he'd done to you. When Aunt Agnes and Uncle Pete found out, they fell into depression. They didn't talk, Stasia. Not for months. It was only on their deathbed that they said something."

"What did they say?" I asked.

"That they hoped to see you again. They loved you so much. Much more than they did me. Perhaps it was because I blamed them for our parents' death."

Nothing in the memories showed me what had happened to my parents. I just realized I wasn't even curious until now.

Fabienne held a little white candle for light. We were still whispering, and the lack of noise felt good and comforted me.

"I think you were so scared of the forest because that's how they died. Right after you were born, Father went into the woods to hunt and he fell into a well. When nightfall came, Mother was so worried she went looking for him. She heard his screams and tried to find him."

"How did she die?"

"She found him. Tried to save him but fell in herself. It was a tragedy. You and I went to live with Aunt Agnes and Uncle Pete shortly after. Because you were younger than I was, you didn't really remember anything. But I remember our parents. I miss them."

"Thanks for telling me," I said as I hugged her. "You'll see them again, Fabienne. You will."

"So did you find it? Did you find the diamond?" she asked, but she seemed to know the answer already.

"Tell me what this stone does," I pulled out the green emerald from my pocket.

"It's healing energy. Only the blessed can use its vast power. You don't have those powers anymore, but combined with the diamond, you can retain them. The diamond must be used for good will only, or else. Or else the entire land will be destroyed."

"I did put the diamond at the top of Blootea volcano, right?"

"You did, with Abe, when you started to change from the negative energy it contained. Take the diamond and the emerald to the Forest of Green Fever. Do you know it?"

Fabienne took me to the window and pointed out the way. "Be careful Stasia. I'm sorry I didn't tell you all this before. In a way I didn't believe it was actually you."

The walk to the forest was a long and dark one. Surritz always looked different at night, making me confused as to which way I was going. The familiar scent of salt in the air reminded me of the first time Pa took me camping at night in St. Michael.

"Lie down in the backseat and close your eyes," he had said as we drove to the secret camping site. When we got out of the car, I'd closed my eyes as he'd led me into the forest. I was scared but I trusted him. The fragrance of fallen leaves combined with the scents of mushrooms and berries. The air was fresh and dewy on my skin. When he had allowed me to open my eyes, I saw that he had already visited the site earlier where he had set up the tent and stacked logs to start a fire. When I looked at him ecstatically, he had responded with the biggest smile I had ever seen on his face.

I missed that smile. The memories attached to it were ones of security and happiness. I didn't feel either right now.

When loud shuffling and coughs caught me off guard, I turned around in the woods unaware of where I'd been heading. In these woods, there were no croaking frogs or shrieking owls. I even missed the buzzing of mosquitoes.

The crunching got louder until someone tapped me on the shoulder. I jumped around swiftly to see Billy standing close to me.

"Where you off to?" he asked happily.

"Exploring… like always," I managed to reply.

"At 11:00 at night?"

"Yes, and what is it that you are doing around at this hour?" I asked him nervously.

He lifted his eyebrows as if he were mocking me. "We are nocturnal, silly girl."

Why had he really come to St. Michael to find me? I didn't want to ask, but the energy inside me pushed out the words before I could even think about forcing them back down.

"Have you ever heard the expression 'Gone with the stones are the one'?" I asked.

A few seconds passed and nothing changed. He looked at the ground, expressionless. In slow motion, air filled his lungs, his mouth opened to speak, and his eyes flicked up to look into mine. I sighed in relief, thinking about how stupid and crazy I had really become. But when I looked up, expecting him to smile, I saw something different.

Before he could answer, his face started to shake and the skin from his head flew off to reveal his skull. Birds flew away squawking. Frightened, I shook my head to regain reality.

"No, what does it mean?" he asked suspiciously.

In the moonlight Billy's eyes glistened red. He was almost as tall as I was when he stood on his hind legs. His two front paws hung close to his chest, his long claws dangled beside his dark feathers.

"It just came to me, in my head, I'm not sure what it means," I lied.

He came closer, and at that point, he was taller. His eyes were bigger, his coat smelled of something rotten, and his voice was deep and raspy.

"The animals, they're waiting," he whispered in my ear.

We glared at each other. We repeated the gesture several times without saying anything. I felt completely comfortable not speaking. He looked away and looked back. Looked away and looked back. Time seemed to be passing quickly again.

I pray that Billy is okay. I pray. I pray. I wish. I want. I don't care what you've done.

The words kept flowing through my mind. It was the only way I could keep from being scared. I didn't care what happened to me anymore.

I just hope Abe is okay. I hope you're okay. I pray for this, to whoever is listening.

"Take this," I said as I pulled out the green emerald from my pocket and put it in his paw. "It heals. Someone once told me that."

Surprisingly, Billy took his eyes away from me. His fangs retracted back into his mouth. His red eyes were dark again.

And out of nowhere, tears streamed out of his eyes. He lowered his head and sobbed. His face filled with tears and he kept sweeping them away with his big paws.

His expression changed to sorrow. "Wow, I feel different. I just feel relieved. Like something was taken out of me," he said. "When I look at you Stasia, I see Nina. I really do. The two of you are starting to blend together, it is so strange."

He continued, "In fact, I knew you very well. You don't even remember me. But why should you? I have been cursed to be able to lie, and now I cannot stop."

While he was speaking, his face started to blend together with someone else's too. I was starting to remember.

"My name, it isn't Billy," he said quietly. "My real name is Toro. Have you heard the name before?"

He looked up at me with large, teary-eyed brown eyes. I suddenly remembered why he looked so familiar.

"Toro?"

"The truth is, I came to find you in St. Michael to make things right. I was given the task of finding you. For Abe. He gave me a chance to be redeemed for what I had done. I was the only other dragon left that could do the job. Because the first dragon for the job, he was captured and killed. He didn't know how to mask his energy on Earth like I have learned."

"What happened to him?"

"He's been put on display."

"Where?" I asked.

"You've seen him. He's in a museum. He was one of the good ones, Stasia."

I gasped when I knew who he was. Suddenly, the memories of my first trip to the museum in St. Michael flashed back into my mind. The smell. The colors. It was Elgor. He had been fished right out of the ocean because he had been trying to protect me.

"But I wronged Abe, again. I have done something terrible. Something that can never be forgiven." Billy said.

This was the first time I saw Billy get down on all fours where he could no longer look me in the eye. His body began to shrink. Soon, he was barely larger than a small cat.

"Tell me," I crouched down next to him to hear what he was saying.

"Don't be scared," he screamed, but I only caught it as a whisper.

I heard Pa's voice in my head. His first words of advice to me about camping: *Animals will always be scared of you if you show them you are not afraid.*

Billy's body started to blink in and out. My vision became blurry as he started to shake. Different colors appeared on his body and his features started to change. His coat turned a lighter green and his eyes a hazel color. A transformation was occurring. When everything stopped, I recognized him as Toro.

"Yes, I did it," he said about killing me, "and I cannot lie any longer, since you learned the truth today. I know you now have the diamond again. Abe wanted me to find you, to tell you he could not get to St. Michael and that you needed to save the animals that died. But I used the opportunity for something else. I used it to try to get you to find the diamond for me, not for the animals. I wanted to have the stone so badly, so I could use the energy to become more powerful myself. It's what I have always selfishly wanted."

"It's true then. Wayters are coming to St. Michael to eat all of us." I said.

"No, Stasia. I already told you, we don't eat. We use energy from the sun to survive. But our ocean is getting colder too. We need another place to inhabit. To co-exist, like on Surritz." He caught my confused expression.

"Stasia, there's someone else that is trying to control Surritz. It's not just me. When Elgor died, Abe reached out to another person he knew you would meet. He tried so hard to contact you before he asked me."

I smiled thinking about how Pa was never able to start a fire in the woods. He always slipped his matches in his pocket and pretended to rub sticks together.

"Are you listening? There is something you don't understand. We all follow each other from lifetime to lifetime. The same people always surround us until we learn to love and help each other. Until we are grateful! There are many on Earth that you have lived with before."

Why wasn't I listening? Because all I wanted was to be back in St. Michael. I wanted to be camping with Pa, or baking cookies with Mama.

Pumpkin Pie? Her silly accent drifted through my thoughts. I missed them. I missed them so much. Those little moments weren't boring at all. They were my life. My precious life with the people who loved me.

"So you can communicate with Abe?" I asked him.

"Only once. He came to me in a dream, told me to find you. I swear I haven't heard from him since. Since he discovered my true intentions. It's true that you can save the animals with that diamond, but you must be careful."

I could see inside Billy's eyes now. They changed from almond shape to round grapes. For the first time I actually did feel his energy. It was sympathy.

Even though it was night and I did not know where I was going, I began to run. My legs took off like they didn't belong to my body. I felt every piece of wet grass slide against my legs. I needed to get to the Forest of Green Fever.

"Stasia!" Billy yelled in the distance.

For the next few hours, I wandered around looking for the magical forest until I began to get so tired my eyelids drooped and my vision became hazy. It was at that moment when I stopped to rest on a tree stump that I saw the forest start to grow out of nowhere. Fluorescent green trees rose right out of the dirt. The flat prairie turned into a luscious, tropical forest. Birds of all sorts sang and I could hear the hooves of animals trotting all around me. Dancing. Only a few feet from my face, I stepped into the exquisite forest and immediately felt the peaceful nature of this divine place. Thick vines hung from trees, swaying in all directions. Flowers bloomed right in front of my eyes. Water trickled down creeks and frogs sang, reminding me of the sweet serenade of tree frogs in St. Michael. Monkeys slept in trees and zebras turned to smile at me, water still dripping from their mouths. Turtles basked on rocks where sunlight danced through the foliage. And in between it all, there was the dance floor. Horses spun silently on two feet like ballerinas. The drummers were elephants, whose feet hit the ground in rhythmic patterns. They all twirled around, occasionally passing right through one another.

I looked back the way I had come to re-orient myself

and saw only darkness.

Where am I? I thought. And the answer was immediately given to me. .

We are the dead.

Welcome to our ballroom.

> *I thought the in-between was a place full of sorrow*, I thought again.

In the distance, an old white horse spoke to me. "This is not the in-between. It's another plane for the ones who have died naturally," he said. "You can access this anytime, when you close your eyes and believe."

His face came closer and closer until his teeth were right up against mine. I grabbed his neck and hugged him, then started to sing. I jumped on his soft back, petting the mane that was perfectly in place.

And then, my eyes opened. I jolted awake. I was still sitting on the rock, shivering. It was dark. There was no one around. The Forest of Green Fever was still a mystery to me, but the breath from the horse's words continued to sting my face. I realized I was standing in the very spot where Abe and Nina had met, the spot where the castle once stood.

CHAPTER 31

OVER THE next couple days, I felt like I spent all my time sleeping. More memories from my childhood came into my mind. I remembered a poem Pa wrote and always recited to me before I went to sleep.

Tonight, as you lay,
Remember,
It doesn't matter what they say.
It's not what they think,
But what you do.
Don't forget,
I'm always here,
I love you.

Pa's voice drifted in and out of my sleep. *You're beautiful. Never forget that, ok?*

Another scene flashed through my mind.

"Hold it like this," he had said as we drifted around in the small dinghy. "It's easy, it's just a rod. When you feel a tug, let me know."

I was barely seven years old, but he was already teaching me to fish.

"What happens when it tugs?" I had asked.

"That means we eat dinner tonight," he teased.

The few times I'd ventured out of Fabienne's house, I hadn't seen Billy. I did not run into Milo or Gito. I didn't hear another word about Abe and even Fabienne had fallen back into depression, refusing to speak.

Time seemed to regress at certain points. At others, it seemed to stand still. Amelie pursued me relentlessly for answers but I had none.

What happened with the diamond?

Where is Abe?

Did you see Billy again?

You SURE he is telling you the truth this time?

I didn't know anything short of whether I was actually living and breathing at that very moment.

"Billy said there's someone else," I finally told her.

"I say we find him and ask him more questions. He's the only one that's talking. You'll never see Abe again unless you start asking questions. And what if he knows something about my mother. Why else would she have come to Surritz?"

We sat in the same tiny room in Fabienne's house. The fire was burning as usual and there were pots of tea on the stove whistling.

"If Billy did apologize, maybe he's telling the truth now," Amelie said. "Maybe he is scared too. Maybe there's danger coming near. You're probably the only one who can stop it. You do have the diamond now."

I wished myself a more interesting and important life and now that I had gotten it, I couldn't wait to go home. I would never complain again that I was bored. I wanted to lie in my bedroom and smell the moldy curtains. I wanted to take a long bath and read my old books. I would give anything to go back to St. Michael and even back to Puncchit and the snow. And the worst part was that I *could* go back. All I needed to do was jump into the funnel, run back through the woods, slip into my bedroom and pretend none of this had ever happened. So why couldn't I do it? What was this longing I had to serve the animals in Surritz? To make things right.

I struggled with the window latch as I decided to sneak out that night and search for Billy. There was no way I was going fit into his front door as he slept during the day, so I knew the only way to find him was to catch him prowling at night. Nighttime was not my favorite in Surritz. It was almost too quiet. The dragons' slinky bodies scared me—half because I knew of their capabilities to lie, and the other half because one of them had killed me. I still did not know what the Forest of Green Fever was or how I could find it. In addition, Fabienne's silence had returned and I could not get any more information from her.

I followed the path along the creek, stopping twice to get a drink of water. I loved putting my hands in the water because of the colors that radiated from them. I watched them dance around my hands before disappearing along with the current. The water was not cold; it was always pleasant. I began to follow the creek, walking beside the edge until I saw that it opened up into a large pond. Hundreds of water lilies perched on top of the water—so many that I could not see the water beneath them. I tried to pick one up but their vines were strongly attached to something at the bottom. Each time I touched one, it opened its petals before angrily snapping them shut again. I played with them touching one and then another until I heard a noise in the distance, the sound of splashing.

"Who—who's there?" a voice broke through the silence.

I turned around and saw the lilies spreading apart as a dark figure glided towards me through the water.

"I saaaaaid—who is there?" it repeated.

"I'm Stasia. I think I'm lost."

"Stasia! Ahhh, hello, very nice to see you again. You have come back. I missed you. How are you? Why didn't you say it was you? Always glad to see you."

"Gito? Is that you?" I asked.

"Yes, my dear. It is me. Me. Me. Me. Don't be afraid. You startled me. You woke me!"

His little whiskers and beak twitched as he came closer, spraying water in all directions. "Well, well, what are you doing up so late my dear? And here by the lake? What are you looking for?"

"I'm just looking... for nothing. I couldn't sleep."

Gito turned onto his back to reveal what I could have sworn was a foot.

"You swim with your tail right?" I asked.

He let out a strange laugh, tilting his head backwards before immediately looking back at me seriously. "No, I have legs."

I laughed now too, and I heard my voice echoing through the volcano.

Gito stared at me, not amused. He tilted his head to the left side and scrunched his eyebrows before coming a little closer to my face. "What's so funny?"

"Well, I just assumed you had no legs."

"Why not? It's just, well, I promised myself I could

tell this story and I will not cry. I will not cry. Gito, do not cry!" He shook his head from side to side and then started hysterically releasing tears right and left. They gently hit the water like drops in a still bath.

"I am not a mean person. I would have taken you to Blootea peak myself. I would have stopped my swimming. I *wanted* to stop my swimming. But it was not because I could not get onto land, it's because I am not *allowed* to get onto land. I love to run. I want to run. I want to exercise my legs in other ways than swimming. Oh! How I loved to run and now I am banned. I cannot run. If I get out, I will die. I am forced to stay in this yucky, murky, disgusting water until my time comes where I will be just as happy to die. But I do not want to kill myself. If I kill myself, I go in the "in-between" where I will repeat my pain and suffering forever. Oh, it will be just dreadful."

"You know of the 'in-between'? So it's true, this place exists?"

"It does exist. Do you know how I know? Because I was there. I was there traveling around in my own sadness for what seemed like eternity. And then, one day, someone saved me. I was brought back. But it seemed nature got it all mixed up because now I am in this strange, ugly, awful, disgusting body." He sobbed again mumbling words I could not decipher. This was the same story Milo told.

"I think you are beautiful. Don't cry. Please don't cry." I said as I touched his face.

"Oh, do you mean it?" He was serious again.

"Yes, I mean it. Can't lie, remember?"

He closed his eyes and smiled. "Oh, I love people from the Care Being. Is that why they call it the Care Being? Because all of your people care?"

I smiled awkwardly. "How long have you been water bound?"

"I was a beautiful, black stallion with two little white spots on my left ear. I could run for miles. This was so long ago. Back then everything was different. Our master, he died. He was killed and we all followed. I could not live without my master. I didn't want to. Surritz was being taken over by..." He stopped, looked around, and then whispered, "Those dreadful dragons. The only ones that can still run free."

"How did you come back?"

"Well it's a very long story but I will give you the abridged version. Oh, it is so long I don't know where to start. Ok, I will just start. A Wayter killed our Master and Lady of Animals and we all just killed ourselves after. I actually chose to run off a cliff. I thought this would probably be the easiest way to die. It was pretty easy. I actually didn't feel it. Not until I got to the 'in-between'. It was so terrible then!"

Gito looked at me completely satisfied with his story.

"You already told me this Gito. I'm wondering how you came back from the 'in-between'."

"Oh, right. Yes. The coming-back story. Ok, this story is not as long. After I had been repeating my sorrow for fifteen years, someone finally picked up my stone. You see, we all have a stone that holds our energy. My stone is an aquamarine. If the right person, with good intentions, finds it and has love in their hearts, I am released. Suddenly, I just found myself back here! However, like I said, I was in this dreadful body. Obviously something did not go right. And when I tried to step on land, one of my legs got shocked. Like ten million volts of electricity ran up my body. I don't think any land animals have come back. They can't. The dragons have booby trapped the island."

I struggled with whether I should say the mantra to him. But after a few minutes I couldn't resist. I closed my eyes telling myself to just breathe before saying, "Gone with the stones are the one."

I peeked through my eyelashes to see Gito's face smiling and coming near me. Only it was his beautiful stallion face.

I embraced this moment that filled me with love and happiness.

"What does it mean? Is that a mantra?" he interrupted.

"It just means you have always lived up to your promises. Everything is going to be alright."

"Oh sweet child of the Care Being. I trust that you are right. Now, what did you say you have come here to look for?"

"Have you ever heard of the Forest of Green Fever?"

"But of course I have heard of such. It would be an honor to visit the Forest of Green Fever! The Forest of Green Fever is a place that only few can see. I have never seen it personally. But I hear it's wonderful!"

He looked around again before speaking very softly. "There are no dragons in there and they cannot access it. It drives them crazy. It is only for the ones with pure intentions! Or, if you have the *stone*."

"It's where I am going," I explained.

Gito's mouth grew wide and he gasped, "Who are you really? How can you access the Forest of Green Fever?"

"If I tell you, you mustn't tell a soul. I know you keep your promises, so will you promise me this—that you will tell no one? Not even Milo?"

"Yes, I promise. Promise! You have my word. Cross my heart and hope to die," he said as he drew an 'x' in the air with his paws.

I let out a sigh of relief. "Ok… I am Nina."

Gito stared at me waiting for me to continue. "Nina who? I know three Nina's and to be quite honest they are not so nice. Although, they are dead now. Actually one of them is in the in-between. Oh, I do feel for her so much, to be around that pain day and night. It is terrible. A shame. Dreadful actually. I shouldn't have said she was mean."

"Gito, I am Nina. Nina, the Lady of Animals. The Nina you killed yourself for. I am in another life now and I am here to rescue you. To recue all the animals."

"It can't be true. Nina did not look anything like you," he gasped and turned away sharply.

I grabbed the right side of my neck where I had the birthmark. But I wasn't ashamed anymore as I thought of how Nina died so I could become who I am.

"And *you* look like the one you once were?"

He started tearing up again before I interrupted. "I need to find the Forest of Green Fever, but I don't know why. I was hoping you could help me."

"The Forest houses all the magical stones. The only place they can be found in Surritz is on the top of Blootea and the Forest of Green fever. When they all are taken back to where they are created, they regain their original powers. See? But they can adapt to negative energy if they get into the wrong hands."

"Thank you Gito. I have one more question. How are Amelie and I able to communicate with you and Milo and the dragons?"

"The energy is all mixed up around here," he said as

he sighed. "I'm basically half an animal and the whole island is in some sort of time warp." He blinked his eyes and smiled hopefully. "I knew you would come back for us. I always believed in you." He flashed his legs and feet from the water. I think the gesture was a sign of good faith, to show that he was telling the truth. But I already knew that; the mantra had not failed me yet.

It was cold that night, and I walked around aimlessly, encountering more strange things in Surritz. The land was always changing; what I thought was just a beautiful, tropical paradise was really a magical realm. The trees changed color as I walked past them, currents suddenly developed as I stepped in puddles, leaves fell on top of my head, and fog rose from the ground. I walked through the parts of Surritz that I could only describe as "dark"—howling developed from nowhere and the ground was black with dirt and old leaves rather than colorful flowers. I heard some shuffling in the bushes; two little animals peered out from the crispy, brown leaves. *Animals!* I thought to myself, only to realize it was just a couple of dragons.

"You again," one said.

"Why are you constantly sneaking around our land? There's nothing here for you," said the other.

I recognized the squeaky voice as the baby dragons I'd encountered earlier by Blootea. The mere sight of them got me angry and intensely scared at the same time.

"You don't even know how dangerous it is here for you," said the first one.

"Wait until you see *her*," they both said in unison. "You will soon. Tonight. Tonight is full-light. Lots of things happen in full-light."

The bushes rustled again and I heard them both

scamper away. Above, the glow fish were so bright I figured full-light was also mating time. They didn't sleep tonight, but were still but swimming in circles; the lights zoomed in all different directions like fireflies in a trapped jar. Even though I knew no animals were in this forest, I felt like there were eyes watching me from all angles. And then I heard the voices.

There you are.
We are waiting.
We miss you.
Nina...
Save us.
We need you.

The voices were nothing above whispers. I continued to walk forward before I realized I must be in the Forest of Green Fever. Everything around me had changed into the deep, haunting color of moss.

Wind blew. Leaves shifted. Ocean rumbled. Colorless stones, depleted of their energy were tossed away in every corner. The trees hung low, creating a canopy above. I could no longer see the glow fish. Vines grew right up my ankles as I passed by. I kept walking as fast as I could until I saw the very tree I first encountered in Surritz—the Tree of Waking Thoughts. I neared the tree, hoping to see the chair, but instead I saw that it was broken. It didn't resemble a chair at all anymore. The long, beautiful branches were missing leaves. It was dying!

"I knew I'd run into you here," a familiar voice said.

CHAPTER 32

EVERY YEAR during the Christmas holidays, my family traveled to Puncchit for vacation. Everything in Puncchit was shut down from the 21st of December until the second of January. Almost seventy-five percent of the city went on vacation because they were such restless people who could not stand being bored. But, for us, our vacation was to visit this big city, even in off-season. The only shops that were open were a couple of bodegas. It was the only time of year that I looked forward to. The energy of the city no longer permeated through the windows and walls of every building. The snow lay quietly on the streets; it was healthy, with few tire marks.

Last year, before Mama came to visit, Pa and I lay on the streets making snow angels. He'd made hot chocolate and we'd walked the long roads together, pretending to be the last two people on Earth.

"Do you remember what I always told you about never being alone," he'd asked when we'd sat down on a fluffy snow-covered fountain.

"Yes, that they are all around us," I answered.

"Who? Remind me."

"Our spirit guides," I'd said, opening my mouth to taste the feather light snowflakes on my tongue.

There had been serenity in this moment. Something I'd never thought about before.

"And what do we do when we need them?" he'd asked...

As far away from Puncchit and Pa as I was at this moment, I remembered the words he'd told me. And, as I looked at the red hair framing her round face, I knew, even in the dark, who was here with me in Surritz.

What do we do when we need them? I heard Pa's words echo through my mind.

"We ask them to help," I said aloud.

As I got closer to the red haired girl, I remembered the first day I met Maisy in school. I remembered her nice words, and her kind smile. We'd spent hours together in Puncchit, learning about water dragons.

"Gone with the stones are the one," I whispered softly at her, only to see Maisy's skull and five black crows, which came rushing out from it.

I was angry. This was my friend. What was she doing here in Surritz?

"This whole thing started for me way before it started for you, Stasia." She ran her fingers over the tree. "When I was young, Abe came to me in a dream. He said he knew you and I were going to meet someday. He tried to contact you, but you would not cooperate. You were so confused as a child. You kept thinking you were still Nina. You didn't know where you were. You made it so hard for him."

She looked exactly like the ordinary, spunky girl I'd met my first year in Puncchit. She did not look like the headless beasts in the ocean, or the crazy monsters I'd seen in my past life.

"He wanted me to tell you that he couldn't get to St. Michael like you could. He'd tried so hard. He wanted to be with you. So he asked that I take you to Surritz to find the diamond. I didn't believe it. I thought it was just a dream. It was only when I came to St. Michael, and you started talking about Surritz, that I thought it might be real. I didn't know about the gems until I felt one that day we were looking for Amelie."

I knew that Abe probably asked Maisy because he knew she lived in Surritz before. I wondered who she was in her past life and why he thought he could trust her.

"I didn't know what Surritz was," she continued. "Abe told me that if Billy couldn't get to me, that it was my duty to take you to meet him, to give Billy the chance to redeem himself. I was your friend, Stasia. I was going to help you. But once I felt that stone, I couldn't believe its power. I could only imagine what the diamond possessed. And, as it turns out, Billy felt the same. I've had to compete with him this whole time."

Then she laughed, making the hairs stand up on my whole body. Greed. I knew those emotions. I had felt them even as Nina.

"The money we can make with these, Stasia. The control we can have. Don't you want to be a part of that?"

"What about Abe?" I interrupted her. "He trusted you. I trusted you."

"He hasn't gone to his next life, but when he does, you will not be able to contact him at all. All his memories will be erased, just like yours were. It's only a matter of time," she sighed. "I guess you already know that when the diamond is connected with all the stones from St. Michael, the souls will be released. But why would you want to do that? It was their choice to kill themselves. You don't want to release all that power. We can do so much with their energy."

I could feel the diamond radiating in my pocket and I couldn't move as she approached. I was paralyzed again.

"Go back to St. Michael. Your family misses you," she said. "Your dad, he thinks you're dead."

What do we do when we need them? Pa's words echoed through my mind again.

"We ask them to help, Pa... Please, whoever is there, help me now," I said aloud.

Maisy grabbed my right arm, trying to put her left hand in my pocket. I wrapped my hand around her left arm, but she was stronger than I was, and I felt her hand inching forward.

"Just give me the diamond," she said, her teeth clenched.

I could feel my face burning and my arm started to shake. Her nails dug into the side of my arm. I wrapped my foot around her leg, trying to throw her off balance, but she stepped forward and applied more force.

"Why are you making this so hard!" she screamed.

"You're not getting the diamond," I said, but she had already managed to shove her hand in my pocket. Suddenly, as her fingers brushed the stone, my life flashed in front of me in a matter of seconds.

Birth. Abe. Mama. Pa. St. Michael. Puncchit. School.

But it slowed down as I was able to view one of my dreams.

It was nighttime and Abe and I were sitting in front of the ocean in Surritz for quite some time before he got up, put his hands together in the middle of the sea and pulled it apart as if he were opening a curtain. The water rolled to the sides and opened to reveal space. Thousands and thousands of stars twinkled in front of our eyes before they quickly starting moving past us as if the atmosphere was rushing by our faces. I saw people and animals and stones and planets rush by at what felt like one thousand miles per hour. I had the desire to jump in to join them but I knew that it was my time to sit on the beach, to just reflect. Once I had this realization, Abe finally turned and spoke to me:

I'm not going to give up on you. After everything that has happened, I still have only love for you Stasia. It's not that I didn't want to meet you in St. Michael. It wasn't the right time. I'm still here with you, and with your mother. Will I be with you again someday? Yes. Look for me.

Look what's happening to the world. The energy.

You have something.

Save them.

Do the right thing.

Before I woke, he said,

You're not going to remember this, you never do. But I'm going to keep trying.

I could see his face clearly now, before my life kept flashing.

Surritz. Maisy. Amelie. Cold. Snow. Starvation. Extinction.

I opened my eyes and shook my head. This was my life? It couldn't be.

I glared deep into Maisy's eyes. In them I saw snow falling on a barren land. But, in the distance, I heard foot-steps.

Billy? His tail radiated red just as I had seen it in St. Michael. He stood far away. So far I could barely see him.

"This will not be my life." Adrenaline suddenly shot through my limbs and I had incredible power. I pushed my arm out of Maisy's grip and grabbed her hand from my pocket before throwing her to the ground. "You're wrong."

She stood still, holding her chest. Her expression was blank and unmoving. But the snow continued falling in her eyes as her pupils became all white.

"Her energy. It's been depleted. Get her to the funnel. We have to send her back." Billy continued, "The diamond is being connected with all the other stones. They are around here somewhere," he explained. "We need to save her. We cannot be like her. Come out of the forest. I will take her to the funnel."

Maisy's body began to shake as I put her around mine and dragged her towards Billy.

"What's going on? Is she dying?" I asked.

She was already stiff and cold.

"She won't if we get her back to St. Michael. She will awake without any memory of this, don't worry. You see, the diamond is the most dangerous of all because it harvests all the worst intentions...but only in the people that produce them."

"The funnel, it's so far. She's already stone cold," I said, panicking.

"You're in the forest of Green Fever, Stasia. Just wish for it. Just as you just did with the stones. All it takes is a thought."

A thought? I didn't know what he was talking about until the words came flowing into my mind again.

Please provide me with the funnel to St. Michael.

Slowly, the Tree of Waking Thoughts became blurry. Faint trickling water turned into rushing waves as the tree morphed into the funnel, folding its branches around itself like a tube.

I placed Maisy on the bottom and she lifted slowly until she was sucked away instantly as the tree reappeared.

"It's done," I said to Billy. "All the stones are here now. I can see them."

Tucked away in the corner where Maisy stood, all the gems glistened.

"The emerald houses the turtles—they provide healing energy. The rubies house the lions—they provide warmth and fire. The aquamarines house the stallions—they provide peace and security," Billy said.

Gito, I thought. *Poor Gito.*

Billy went down the list of stones pointing to each and naming the corresponding animal.

"They live in harmony, the stones and the animals. They feed off of each other's energy. That is why we need nature just like we need animals."

"What's your stone?" I asked Billy. "What do the dragons have?"

"We don't have a stone. That's why we tried to take over the land years ago. Jealousy took over the species. Our rock was taken from us. Today it's nothing but granite; set so far into the volcano that we cannot even see it. We will never be free from bad intentions because of what we did. Even our little ones have it."

"Billy, we can all be forgiven if we forgive ourselves," I said, and although I had never thought about that in my life before, I just knew it to be true.

"I believe you, and this is what we must do now," he instructed. Place the diamond and the bag of stones in the groove in the Tree of Waking Thoughts. Together, they will manifest all the memories of life as it once was. The animals that killed themselves will come back. But, be aware, Abe will not come back Stasia. Only the ones in the in-between."

I nodded as I picked up the colorful stones.

"I have to tell you one more thing," Billy said. "When I said that you were in a new life with none of your powers, that wasn't true. You have something very special. See, we never completely lose control of our 'gifts', no matter how our energy transforms. Give me your hand."

He stood up and motioned for me to come to him. He held out his paws and I gently placed my fingers on top of them. He pulled them down to the murky puddle and placed them in the water. Many different colors left my fingertips and bounced around the water, turning it into a bright shade of red.

"*This* is very special. One day you will realize the gift that you have of transferring energy. Practice. Develop it. You have so much more than you know."

I was glad to have the same gift Abe once had. Billy and I exchanged glances but neither of us smiled. He watched as I placed each stone in the tree. I said a prayer for each one before I pulled out the diamond and placed it in the middle.

Slowly, the branches started to pull themselves upright, revealing the light of dawn that peeked through. Leaves of all colors grew out of them. Flowers popped up from every angle and then small and large animals came into my view, flickering at first and then becoming as real as anything I'd ever seen. Lizards ran on the ground and monkeys hung from the trees. Sheep grazed and a herd of white stallions stampeded through, running as fast as they could. A stream of water hit my feet as it rushed down the lush forest. The land was transformed into a beautiful rainforest. The energy was rebalanced and I felt like I was seeing the real land for the first time. The land I remembered so well.

Animals stared at me as they walked by, but I could not communicate with them. I tried again but no one responded.

"Billy, why are they not answering?" I stared at Billy's round, dark eyes.

He was silent. Even Billy, who stood right next to me, no longer spoke. We stood for some time looking into each other's eyes until he, too, took off and scampered away with the rest of the animals. I said a prayer for him as well, hoping that someday he could be forgiven for what he'd done.

"I'm not Nina anymore," I said aloud before I turned to walk out of the Forest of Green Fever.

I took my time walking back to Fabienne's house. More and more animals were flying, grazing, sleeping and eating. Surritz was full of creatures.

"Why are you up so early?" I asked Fabienne as I returned to see her cooking in the kitchen.

"I woke up early feeling refreshed. I feel so good today. I haven't felt this way in a long time," she said.

"Is Amelie awake?" I called rushing upstairs to get her before Fabienne could answer. "It's time to go," I said as I opened the door to find her already packing. "Where are you going?"

"I looked out the window this morning and saw a pack of wild geese grazing by the pond. On the land! Mind you, the pond looked a lot more beautiful than it had before. And the geese. They were such a strange sight. I just can't pinpoint why." She smiled at me.

"I'll explain later. But, we have to get back to St.

Michael. It's time."

"Looks like someone had a long night… and has a lot of storytelling to do."

I packed the few items I had. I tried to get used to the fact that I was probably leaving Surritz forever. I didn't know if I'd even be able to return once I went back to St. Michael.

"Fabienne," I said, walking down the stairs, "Amelie and I have to get back to St. Michael. Thank you for everything. You've been nothing but kind to us."

"I'm so glad to see you again, and that you're okay. I spent years trying to find your body. We knew, but we didn't know where." Tears ran down her cheeks. All the emotions I had never seen this entire time came pouring out.

"It was in the castle, below where everyone was buried. Down the spiral stairs in the back. I'll miss you so much Fabienne."

I was rushing. I knew it was time to get home, and I couldn't wait. I missed Mama and Pa so much. I wanted them to know that I was alive. That I was going to be alive for a long time.

"Goodbye, Stasia. I'll think of you," said Fabienne.

As we walked away from the house and towards the ocean, I turned around to wave goodbye to Fabienne. It was then that I saw her bend down and start petting a black stallion that showed up at her front door. One that was friendly with two little white spots above his left ear.

CHAPTER 33

IT HAD been five months since Amelie and I returned to St. Michael. Mama had finally forgiven me recently for disappearing for months, even though she still didn't believe where I'd gone. I think she got tired of the screaming and yelling, tired of the scolding, tired of the days that passed that she refused to speak to me. But it was Pa's reaction that touched me. He cried. He hugged me, consoled me, and told me that he would listen if this was really something important to me. I even felt comfortable enough to tell him some stories about how I was able to speak to needlefish. I finally reminded him of the first time he showed them to me and how much happiness that experience had brought me.

"Let's snorkel again. I have lots more to show you," was all he had said.

We were in the middle of summer now. Pure, intense colors were everywhere. Endless variations of blue in the sea and sky contrasted with bright reds, yellows, and oranges of hibiscus, bougainvillea, and flamboyant. Exotic scents frangipani and jasmine mixed with spicy salt spray to produce such a pleasing effect to the senses. Something in the air was different when the weather changed. It always felt thicker. The humidity soaked through my skin and released some life back into my body.

Life in St. Michael was exactly how I remembered it as a child. From my window, I watched many colorful boats sailing by. Cows and goats walked past the roads during the day and the crickets and tree frogs sang happily in the night. Palm trees were back to their erect position and in full bloom. They even had fresh coconuts!

On the beaches, parents watched as their children wrestled with the waves and built castles in the sand. The market place was full of strangers from far away who wanted a taste of the Caribbean. Life was back to normal. But, there were two things I hadn't forgotten about—the diamond in the bottom of my dresser, and the fact that Pa was not my real father.

Today I headed over to Amelie's house. The walk was pleasant; there was a warm breeze and finally I was able to wear my old beach clothes. My flip-flops squeaked as I walked up the steep hill. I had the accompaniment of birds and lizards. The view from the hill was one thing I could never forget. Boats the size of figurines swayed in the blue ocean below. I could barely make out people sunbathing on the beaches. It was summer now, but the dead trees that did not bloom reminded me that winter would come again soon. Now that I knew global cooling was caused by our hateful thoughts and emotions, what could I do to reverse this shift in the energy on Earth? Was Abe going to help me?

Dr. Rose let me into the house and motioned to the porch where Amelie was sitting. Seeing Dr. Rose was still awkward, but he had agreed with Pa that he would not bring up anything "from my past". In other words, 'from the folder.' He was friendly and offered me some water before I opened the back door.

"Hey you," I said, eyeing Amelie's multi-colored romper. "That's an interesting choice of clothing."

She laughed. "I know you love it."

Amelie and I had developed a different kind of relationship once we returned from Surritz. I understood her better and she valued my opinions. I even valued my own opinions.

Amelie rose from her chair as I started to sit in mine. "I know what it means," she said. "Sit down and write. The words from the apparition."

"What does it mean?" I asked her. We had tried desperately to figure it out, but we never could.

"Have you ever heard of automatic writing?" she asked.

"No," I said.

"Oh, Stasia, I cannot thank you enough!" She hugged me the same way she did months ago when I first got back to St. Michael. "You've changed my life. You have."

"What is it, Am?"

"Automatic writing is when a spirit tries to contact you through writing. Some people have this gift."

"How does it work?" I asked her.

"I've been practicing. I sit down with a piece of paper and a pencil. I start to meditate and if I am open enough, a spirit writes through me. Takes my hand and moves it to create words. Look…" She reached for a folded piece of paper on the table. Her eyes welled up with tears. "Read it. It's from her."

I unfolded it quickly to see sentences in a loopy script.

Amelie –

Now you know your gift, and what a great one it is to have. I am always here with you; all you have to do is think my name. I know you have wondered, for so long, about Surritz. It is where I once lived in my previous life. I was checking up on my daughter, Fabienne. She was alone when I died.

I tried to reach you through the Ouija board, but someone else came through first, Billy. Those tricky Wayters... I am in a happy place. Someday I will tell you where you go when you die. Use your gift wisely. Inform people of theirs. And never forget to love.

That's all for now.

Un Bisous

    Ma

"Amelie, is it real? Is it true about Fabienne? That means your mother was mine in my past life!"

"I know it's strange but there's no other way I could know this information. We *are* kind of like sisters, don't you think?"

"So it was you who was moving the planchette! Not Flynn!" I teased.

"Ironic right, but I didn't know!"

"Guess you did me a favor. If that hadn't happened, I would have never figured out what was going on. Did you tell your dad about your mom?"

"Not yet. Still contemplating it. By the way, do you miss Puncchit?" Amelie asked, her body now curled up on the lawn chair.

"I'm so glad my dad is back in St. Michael."

"Come on, you gotta miss the Brooderkaas?" she

giggled.

"Pa's actually talking about opening BreadBar here!"

"Good, now I can be the judge of whether they *really* are as good as you say! I guess you still haven't heard from Maisy or Flynn right?"

They hadn't been on St. Michael when we'd returned. Pa had said that they'd left to go back to Puncchit. I wondered if Maisy remembered anything that had happened. I wondered how she got to Surritz. Who was she in her past life? But, even though I wondered about Maisy, it was Flynn who I missed.

THAT NIGHT, as I sat by the pool with Mama, listening to the music blare from the beach bar below our house, she confessed that even though Pa was right there when I was born, he was not my biological father.

"Who is?" I asked having never heard her side of the story.

"His name was Arlo," she said rather quickly. "He was in St. Michael for a short time. Right before I met your father."

"And no one knew him?"

"The population back then was very small."

"No one, Mama? It was just you and Arlo on the island?"

After a short pause, she answered, "The only other person that met him was Mr. Gordon."

So that's why I always had a strange feeling around Mr. Gordon. He knew Abe when he was in St. Michael. He must know that I was his daughter.

"Why did he leave you?" I asked Mama.

I had a feeling that the conversation would not go

much further. Why did Mama feel the need to tell me? Had she had some kind of inkling that I had just found out anyway?

But instead of answering, she pulled out the black and white photographs Flynn had been looking at in the den.

"This is him," she pointed to Abe, who looked completely different with a beard.

And beside him was me as Nina, and Fabienne, and Abe's parents, and Toro! But Mama didn't know that.

"He gave me these photos. Said these people were very important to him. He missed them."

As I looked closely at the photos, I did recognize myself as Nina. There was some water damage, but what I thought was a dog had actually been Toro.

"Who did he say they were?" I asked her.

She thought for a moment in a sort of confusion. "I never found out. He never really told me. But I got the sense that they might be family."

I ran my fingers over the evidence that revealed my life in Surritz. I was not going to share my secrets with Mama. She would never understand the fact that she was the woman I was jealous of, and how I willed myself to be her daughter to be closer to Abe. It seemed crazy just thinking about it. Because now, all I was, was just me, Stasia.

"Unfortunately, I don't know a lot about your real father, but I know if he were here he would have cared for you deeply. He was an old soul. He had many secrets. But I was okay with that."

I understood. He always had a lot of secrets. He was smart, but awkward. Happy but tormented at times. His behavior was hard to decipher. But I still felt confident that he would keep trying to contact me.

After Mama went inside, I stretched out to hang my head over the top of the lawn chair. My hair swept the ground and I felt the blood rush to my temples.

The tropical, humid night was full of sounds. My trained ears heard the goats and cows that were grazing in the grass, the crickets that burped on the roadside, and the frogs that rustled in the trees.

Boom. Boom. Boom.

All I care for is you. I live my life the way I want to.

The lyrics from the lady singing at the bar were extraordinarily clear and superseded any of the other background noises. For the first time in months, actually years, my mind was clear. I wasn't confused or scared or sad or even happy. I was just content.

Until now, I never understood that part of life was not understanding it. That we can't plan everything, or know everything, or want everything. It was about believing that someone out there was looking out for us, planning our next move for us. Telling us to trust our instincts and that it was okay to feel insecure. To just let go.

Maybe that's what kept me going, what kept me fighting to learn more.

I breathed in the salty air and stretched out on the warm chair. My body automatically swayed with the beat, and I couldn't stop thinking about Flynn's smile.

When I was starting to fall asleep, I found myself wandering into the attic, the room that made me feel the most comfortable, in the home that I finally loved. I sat on the ground, drifting away, until I heard the gurgling sounds of my alarm clock. The water circled up and around until it came trickling down the colored rocks splashing into the pond below. Sleep did not affect its function now. It ran like a runner in a race, smooth and steady, dedicated to the same action over and over without tire, before it shut off completely, satisfied with its performance.

My eyes closed. Finally there was silence...until slowly I heard the bass drum. The laughter. The swoosh of air passing quickly between beings. Even with my eyes closed, I could see all the love around me in shapes of not only animals, but a man too. He knew them so well; he danced the same way they did.

I lay on the wooden floor as my mind drifted farther and farther away, until the peaceful sounds put me into a deep sleep.

ABOUT THE AUTHOR

Nicola Mar grew up on the Caribbean island of St. Maarten, where she wrote her first short story at age seven. At eighteen, Nicola moved to the U.S. to continue her education, graduating from Rollins College with a bachelor's degree in anthropology and a specialty in creative writing. After spending many years in the fashion industry, Nicola chose to pursue her writing full-time. She currently lives in New York City with her two dogs. Visit her website at www.nicolamar.com